Also in the *X Libris* series:

# Rough Trade

Emma Allan

**LIBRIS**

An *X Libris* Book

First published by X Libris in 1997

A CIP catalogue record for this book
is available from the British Library.

ISBN 0 7515 2045 4

Photoset in North Wales by
Derek Doyle & Associates, Mold, Flintshire
Printed and bound in Great Britain by
Clays Ltd, St Ives plc

X Libris
A Division of
Little, Brown and Company (UK)
Brettenham House
Lancaster Place
London WC2E 7EN

# Rough Trade

# *Prologue*

---

*IT WAS HER* birthday. It was June. It was hot. Very hot. Hot and humid. The sun was high and there wasn't a single cloud in the sky.

A party had been planned for that night. All her friends would be there. But her *best* friend, Andrea Hamilton, had asked her to go for a bike ride in the afternoon, down to the small lake they had found, their secret place. The water was fed from some underground aquifer and was always cold. It would be delicious to swim on such a day.

The ride made them hot and sweaty. Abandoning their bikes under a huge horse-chestnut tree, its shade extending out over the water's edge, they pulled off their T–shirts and shorts, kicked off their socks and trainers and dived, naked, into the water.

They swam for hours, or so it seemed, then lay on the grass under the broad-leafed tree, shaded from the sun. And that's when it happened. She could never remember how exactly, whose hand had stroked the other's body, or whose lips had brushed the other's mouth, as though it were the most natural thing in the world to do. Nor who

1

had been the first to cup one of their burgeoning breasts, tease a nipple to stiffness and pinch it with a playfulness that soon turned to deadly earnest. She did remember, as vividly as she remembered anything else that had happened in her life, that it was Andrea who had snaked her hand down over her belly and whose finger had probed into her labia, experimentally at first, then stroked between them.

From that moment on, however, the hesitant fumblings became more assured. As pleasure turned to passion, as the nascent feelings developed into strong sensations, she was shocked at the power her arousal could generate.

Andrea led the way. She was tall and slender and knowing. Her long blonde hair swept her friend's body as she came up on to her knees and began kissing her breasts, her hands running down her legs, caressing the incredibly soft, silky flesh of her inner thighs. She pulled them gently apart to expose the scarlet furrow of her sex. She dipped her head and kissed it as though it were another mouth, her lips squirming against it, her tongue darting out to lap at the sweet, copious nectar with which it was already flooded.

But despite the onslaught of pleasure this produced, where Andrea led she wanted to follow. She twisted around and wriggled her head between Andrea's thighs, so her sex, covered in a bush of hair so light and fluffy it looked like down, was poised above her.

Then they were joined. A wave of feeling engulfed them both as Andrea lowered her sex on to her friend's mouth, an invisible connection made between them, a circuit completed. What Andrea did to her, she mimicked; unimagined

2

things, but exciting, almost too exciting. They licked and sucked and stroked each other's sexes with their tongues, using the same tempo. But as the feeling mounted in their bodies, the rhythmic tremors of instincts yet to be fully shaped soon demanded more. Only Andrea knew what to do, only she knew to move her tongue to the little almond sized promontory at the top of her friend's labia. Soon they were locked together, moaning, squirming, dancing with passion, every lingering sensation, every new nuance of feeling increasing their need, building to a crescendo.

She was not naive. She had experienced fumbled sexual longing before with boys; fevered embraces and guilty touches. But nothing like this, nothing as serious, as meaningful, as affecting. This took over her whole body with a pounding rhythm that got faster and more furious, bringing her to the edge of an abyss then plunging her over it. She clung to Andrea for support, the feeling of the blonde's own climax fuelling her own.

When it was finally over, when they had rolled off each other and lay on the long grass gazing up at the shafts of sunlight trying to filter through the filigreed canopy of leaves, she had no regrets. Andrea was still her best friend. But though she could still taste the sweet juices of the blonde's sex and her own body still ached with the aftermath of passion, she knew she would never do what they had just done again.

blond, curly hair and very blue eyes.

# Chapter One

---

*EVERY DAY FOR* a week. The same routine. First thing in the morning after she'd dressed and made-up. She felt ashamed of herself. She felt like a guilty schoolgirl, hiding behind the lace curtains of her bedroom window so she could see but not be seen. She couldn't help herself. It was hot and after only a few minutes of digging he would strip off his shirt. His legs were already exposed, by jeans cut off at the top of his thighs.

Clare Markham had never seen a body like it, which is why it fascinated her. His chest was broad, his abdomen flat and delineated by hard, stringy muscles, his biceps bulging as he worked. He was tall with long legs which were contoured by thick, well-defined muscles, his whole body like some relief map of musculature. His buttocks were small and tight and hard, like two cantaloupes wrapped in denim.

But it wasn't only his physique that proved so magnetic. He was handsome too. He had short, blond, curly hair and very blue eyes, under a rugged brow. He had a small, straight nose, sharp, high cheekbones and a square jaw. She noticed he had small, very delicate ears.

He had arrived with the other builders on the first day that work had begun.

Clare had decided to have her house extended. She wanted a new kitchen to replace the small, poky room she used at the moment, and a new bathroom that would be en suite with her bedroom. The one could be conveniently constructed above the other. Two months ago she had been promoted to Managing Director of KissCo UK and the alterations were a sort of present to herself. The firm of builders she was using had been recommended by a friend who had been more than satisfied with similar work they had carried out for her.

Reluctantly Clare tore herself away from the bedroom window. The foundations were nearly in place and once they started knocking into the back wall to which the extension was being attached, she would not have such a good vantage point. For one thing she'd have to move into the front bedroom. Her daily routine would have to change.

Checking her appearance one last time in the mirror, she adjusted her short black hair with a single sweep of her fingers and marched downstairs.

'Morning, Mrs Markham,' George Wickes said politely, although he continued to insist that Clare was married, no matter how many times she told him she was not. 'Just making sure everything's going well. Sorry about the mess. Inevitable I'm afraid.' George Wickes was the head of the firm of builders and had arrived every morning to inspect the work. He was a large, avuncular man with heavy jowls and a ruddy complexion, the veins on his face very close to the surface. He had eyes like a basset-hound and, like Stan Laurel, seemed to take an extraordinarily long time to blink, as if the effort of raising his eyelids was too much for him. Even in the hot weather he wore a tweed sports coat with leather patches on the elbows.

'Going to be worse when they knock through,' Clare said.

'Yes, but we'll do that at the last possible minute. Less disruption that way.'

The whole of the ground floor, including the sitting room and dining room, had been stripped of furniture and sheeted with plastic. The carpets had been taken up and scaffolding boards laid on the floor as a path for the wheelbarrow loads of rubble dug out of the back garden, and the hard core that had to replace it.

'Morning, Mrs Markham.' The blond was coming towards them from the back, wheeling a barrow piled high with soil.

'Morning, Gary,' Clare said, her eyes inevitably dropping to the contours of his chest. Perspiration had run down his collar bone, carving a trail in the dirt and dust that caked his skin. The trail ended at the waistband of the sawn off jeans, the denim darker there where it had soaked up the sweat. Clare tore her eyes away, not wanting to be caught staring at his crotch. His muscles rippled as he manoeuvred the heavy load past her.

Leaving George Wickes to get on with his inspection she took her car keys out of her bag and followed Gary outside. He wheeled the barrow up a plank to the top of a large skip parked outside her house, and dumped the contents.

'Nice car,' he said as he headed back down and

saw Clare unlocking her 5 series BMW. He wiped the sweat off his brow with his forearm. He was looking at her, not the silver-coloured car. Clare was not tall, no more than five foot two in her bare feet, and Gary seemed to tower over her.

'Goes with the job,' she said, wishing she had the courage to say what was really on her mind and knowing she never would.

'Nice job, then,' he said. He had a strong South London accent.

Their eyes met. He smiled at her. It was a wistful smile. She wondered if he had ever entertained thoughts about her as graphic as the ones she'd had about him in the last few days.

'Are you working late tonight?' Gary was always the first to arrive and the last to leave.

'Yeah.'

'See you later, then,' she said cheerily, getting into the car. She started the engine but could not resist staring at those taut buttocks, each one a neat handful, as he wheeled the barrow back into her house.

For some reason traffic was light and it took Clare no more than fifteen minutes to drive from her house in Kensington to Grosvenor Square. She parked her car in the underground car park of KissCo's offices, one of only three employees allowed to do so, and took the lift up to her office. It overlooked a corner of the square and the hot weather had already brought people out on to the grass, men stripping off their shirts, women furtively hitching up their skirts to expose the maximum amount of leg to the sun's rays. None of the half a dozen men she could see stretched out on the grass had a physique to rival Gary's.

The phone on her desk rang before she'd had a

chance to sit down.

'Call from Houston,' Janice, Clare's secretary, said with the appropriate foreboding in her voice. Houston was the company headquarters and calls or correspondence from there often resulted in a great deal of extra work for Clare and her team.

'It's a bit early.' Clare sat down at her high-backed, leather swivel chair and looked at her watch. It was five to ten, which meant it was five to four in the morning in Houston.

'The early bird,' Janice joked.

'Put it through.'

The line clicked. 'Ms Markham. I have Bridget Goldsmith on the line for you.'

The line clicked again. 'Clare, good morning.'

'Ms Goldsmith, you're up early.'

Bridget Goldsmith was the President and Chief Operating Executive of KissCo worldwide. Clare was not at all surprised to get a call from her at such an early hour. The rumour in the company was that Bridget never slept.

'I've decided to come to London, Clare,' she said, getting right to the point.

'Oh?'

'The European launch is set for when?'

'First of September.'

'That's just over three months. I think I should come and have a look see before then. I'm going to schedule a trip to Paris too.'

'To see Claude,' Clare said coolly.

'Should be swinging by in, say, two weeks. I'll fax you the actual schedule when it's confirmed. Meantime can you work up a presentation for me. The ad agency, the marketing people. I want to review everything.'

'We're already in the process of combining a

9

presentation.'

'Good.'

'Is there a problem?' The European launch was to be KissCo's biggest marketing operation outside America. A whole new range of cosmetics was to be targeted at every major European country at the same time, with an integrated advertising campaign.

'No, no problem. I just want to have a look. My thinking on this is that it might be better to co-ordinate the launch from Paris.'

'I see.' Clare saw exactly. Claude Duhamel, the managing director of the French subsidiary, had recently returned from a visit to Houston. He had obviously not missed the chance to cast doubt on Clare's competence to handle such a large and expensive operation.

Clare's promotion had been sudden and unexpected. Usually all senior staff up for such important positions were shipped to Houston for extensive evaluations. But KissCo's UK managing director had been poached by a rival company and there had been no time. Clare, as the second most senior person, had been the only possible replacement. Claude had no doubt made capital out of the fact that she had not been properly vetted.

'Don't worry about hotels. We'll do it all from here.'

'Anything else you want?'

'I'll call you if I think of anything. Bye for now.' Having dropped the bombshell Bridget sounded cheery.

Clare put down the phone and began making notes. Janice peered in through the door. She was a plump, short woman who wore knitted twinsets whatever the weather. In combination with her tightly permed, rather thin, brown hair, they made her look at least ten years older than she actually was.

'Can I help?' she asked.

'Yes. Come in.'

They spent the next hour setting up meetings with all the departmental heads to advise them of Bridget's visit and instruct them what would be needed for it. The presentation they were working on would have to be a great deal more detailed if it was going to be made to Bridget in person rather than sent out to Houston by courier.

It was about an hour later when the phone on Clare's desk rang again. This time it was her private line.

'Clare Markham,' she said answering it herself.

'Clare, it's David. How are you?'

'Could be better,' she said, rather abruptly.

'We're still on for tonight, aren't we?' She heard the worry in his voice that something might have come up which she would use as an excuse not to see him.

'Yes, of course.' Actually seeing David Allston tonight was the last thing she really wanted to do, but she didn't have the heart to disappoint him. David's attitude to their relationship was like that of a small child with a new toy. She couldn't bare to snatch it away from him, however much she would have preferred to have an early night and curl up with a good book.

'Great. Do you want to have dinner?'

'I can't cook. My kitchen's been ripped out, remember?'

'Shall I book a table at The Ivy?'

11

'No, no. Nothing like that. I'm not in the mood to get dressed up. The local Italian will do.' Bearing in mind what David would inevitably demand from her after they'd eaten, going to the Italian restaurant she frequented just off Kensington High Street seemed to involve the least effort after what was undoubtedly going to be an exhausting day.

'OK. Eight, then? Is that all right?' She could hear the excitement in his voice. The child had been given his toy again: now, she knew, he would spend the rest of the day planning what games to play with it.

It had been a long day. Every time Clare had arrived home since the building work had begun Gary had still been busying himself in the back, usually on his own, his two other workmates long gone. But tonight Clare was late and he too had gone. The house felt empty. She missed the banter they usually shared.

It was already seven thirty. She went upstairs to the bathroom at the front of the house, stripping off her black suit as she went. In the new bathroom she would have a separate shower cubicle with a powerful shower, but at the moment she had to make do with the shower attached to the mixer taps of the bath and a glass screen at the side of it to prevent the water splashing over the floor. She adjusted the temperature to lukewarm, pulled off the rest of her clothes and stood in the rather sluggish stream, allowing the water to wash over her.

As she closed her eyes and turned her face into the water she thought of Gary, his hard body covered with sweat. She wondered what it would feel like against her. She had had a variety of men in her life and some had been moderately fit, but she'd never had anyone like him, someone whose muscles looked as though they had been shaped in stone by a sculptor. She imagined wrapping her arms around him, hugging him, feeling his strength. The thought made her shudder.

She washed herself quickly, dried herself on a large white towel and cleaned her teeth. In her bedroom she chose a cream and pink patterned cotton dress with a V-neck and cool short sleeves. Though it had a full skirt it was split to well above the knee and showed a lot of her slender, shapely legs. Just as she finished her make-up the doorbell rang.

'You're very punctual,' she told David as she opened the front door. David was always very punctual. Punctiliously punctual. She couldn't help wishing he wasn't.

'Sorry,' he said, kissing her on both cheeks and looking shamefaced.

'I've just got to get my bag,' she said.

'Place looks like a bomb's hit it.'

'Worse to come yet.'

She grabbed her handbag, took out her keys, set the alarm and double-locked the front door. David's burgundy-coloured Bentley was parked behind the builder's skip. He opened the passenger door for her then got behind the wheel.

'Sure you don't want to change your mind about the venue?'

'No,' she said emphatically.

They dined without fuss, ordering only one course and a single bottle of red wine. Clare had the impression that her lack of appetite suited David perfectly. He was impatient for the meal to end.

She had met David Allston at one of KissCo's parties held to launch some new product or other, but she had never discovered why he'd been invited. She guessed, since he was the sort of person constantly pictured in the gossip columns of *Queen*, *Tatler*, and even *Vogue*, KissCo's public relations department had thought his presence might attract a photo opportunity in some such magazine, although on this occasion, at least, they had been disappointed.

David Allston was, in fact, Viscount Bonmouth, the eighth Viscount in a succession dating back to 1781. He looked the part. He was slim – even thin – with a beautifully tailored suit from the firm in Saville Row that had catered to his family for one hundred and fifty years, serving his father and his father's father. His white cotton shirt was from a shirtmaker's in Jermyn Street, who'd also served three generations of Allstons, and his hand-lasted shoes were from Loebbs. He had neatly cut brown hair and a fine, delicately boned face, with a narrow straight nose, and hollow, almost feminine cheekbones. His eyes were light green and oddly nondescript, shallow set and small though he did have the longest eyelashes Clare had ever seen.

His manner suggested his pedigree too. There was a poise about him and an innate elegance that meant no matter how he was sitting or standing he seemed to be perfectly in equilibrium. A little too perfectly sometimes, as his grace could be seen to border on the effeminate. His attitude was not haughty, however. He was not the sort of aristocrat who had seen everything and done everything and was bored with life. He was more like a clever and enquiring child, ready to take on new experiences. And, like a child, he could be very determined to get his own way.

'So when does the big boss arrive?' David asked, as Clare told him of Bridget Goldsmith's decision.

'Two weeks.'

'I'm sure it'll all be fine,' he said. He had never shown much interest in her work or work in general. As far as Clare knew he didn't do much more than see that the family 'pile' in Hertfordshire was kept in good order. He certainly hadn't ever worked for a living and she imagined that it was hard for him to understand the exigencies of the daily grind.

'Do you want coffee?' he asked in a manner that suggested he hoped she would say no. He would have loved merely to have told her to get ready to leave but years of breeding had dictated that in social situations his own needs and desires should never be allowed to take precedence over those of anyone else, particularly those of a woman. From an early age, David had been indoctrinated that, according to the scheme of things, women existed to be cherished and adored, though, of course, they were not necessarily to be taken very seriously.

'Not really,' she said.

'Me neither,' he said, as if they were sharing a secret.

He summoned the waiter and paid the bill with alacrity, hustling her out of the restaurant and into the car as quickly as he dared. The drive to his house was accomplished largely in silence, Clare finding she was in no mood for small talk.

The Allston family's London residence was in a Nash terrace in Regent's Park; it was a corner house with large rectangular windows, curved side walls and a grandiose, stucco-fronted façade with a portico. In square-sided wooden planters, pollarded, ball-shaped bay trees stood on each side of the black, panelled front door.

'Would you like a drink?' David asked, as they walked through the large vestibule, where a huge crystal chandelier hung from a domed ceiling above a black-and-white chequered marble floor.

'Yes. A brandy would be nice.' She needed a brandy to fortify herself, the moment of truth approaching rapidly.

He led the way into the sitting room, where large oatmeal–coloured sofas were arranged around a large fireplace, its grate currently occupied by an arrangement of dried flowers. Normally, she knew, drinks would be provided by the butler, who divided his time between the London and country houses, but on this occasion David went to a large, walnut cocktail cabinet and poured the brandy himself, not wanting to summon the butler from the Stygian depths of the house.

He handed her the drink. She was standing by the window, looking out at Regent's Park.

'Cheers,' he said.

'Nothing for you?'

'No. Not in the mood.'

An air of expectancy hung between them like autumn fog. He was watching her every movement, like a dog waiting for its master to get up and take it for a walk. She knew exactly what he wanted her to do to initiate the complicated ritual that had developed between them. Some nights she would tease him, delay the inevitable, make him wait. But tonight she was too tired for that. She swigged down half the brandy, which she discovered she didn't really want, and put the glass down on a French, Hepplewhite-design, mahogany card table.

'Would you excuse me for a few minutes, darling,' she said, trying to keep the weariness out of her voice.

The look of relief on his face was obvious. 'Of course.'

'I won't be long.'

As she turned to walk towards the door he caught her hand and pressed it to his cheek. 'You're very special,' he said, kissing her fingers.

As she walked up the grand, sweeping staircase and along the corridor to his bedroom, she wondered if it were true. Was she special? How many other women had agreed to participate in David's demands for stylised, ritualistic sex? Perhaps countesses, baronesses and duchesses were used to such things. Or perhaps not. It was entirely possible that she was the first woman who had indulged David's fantasies in this way.

She pushed open the bedroom door, knowing exactly what she would find. There, on the large double bed, the counterpane and bedding already removed, were two beautifully wrapped boxes, one large and rectangular, the other small and square, one on top of the other. Both were wrapped in bright gold foil with gold ribbon.

Clare closed the bedroom door firmly. It had to be closed. She walked over to the bed. Tossing the smaller box aside she sat on the white linen undersheet and ripped the ribbons off the large box. She delved into the layers of white tissue paper. Her hands lighted on something soft and silky. She held it up, the tissue paper falling away. It was a pink body, beautifully and expensively made in the finest silk, with lace insets over the bosom and at the hips. There was a matching pink suspender belt in the box too, and a pair of very sheer, white stockings. There was also a white lace garter. And the letter of course, right at the bottom of the box.

She got to her feet and stripped off her dress, panties and bra, then clipped the suspender belt around her waist. She slipped into the body. The silk was so soft and sensual she felt a flush of sexual pleasure. Her nipples puckered instantly. She glanced into the mirror on the opposite wall. It was a perfect fit. David had a list of all her measurements. The pink suited her dark colouring and the tightness of the garment showed off her figure. She had a good figure, her breasts firm and round and high, her waist narrow, her hips generous but not flabby. The lace over her breasts was transparent and she could see her quite large, rose-red nipples under it. The legs of the body were cut high and its crotch was thin, not quite covering the whole curved plane between her legs but leaving the flesh on either side of her labia clearly visible. Her pubic hair was black and, though not particularly thick, formed a definite dark shadow under the pink silk.

Sitting on the bed she took the stockings out of their cellophane packet and rolled them, one by one, up her slender legs. The suspenders were too long and each had to be adjusted until they held the stockings taut. She spread the elasticated garter between her fingers and inserted her left foot into it, drawing it up her legs until it banded her thigh just below the white welt of the stocking.

At least, she thought, this was underwear she would be able to wear outside the bedroom. So often the boxes David had left on the foot of the bed had contained more outrageous items – cupless bras and crotchless panties, tiny, incredibly tight, red-satin waspies with long ruched suspenders, or patent leather high-heels that had forced her foot up almost vertically. They were all the stuff of his highly developed fantasies, leaving her body decked out like that of some cheap whore.

Smoothing the sheer, white stockings up over her legs, satisfying herself that they were wrinkle free, Clare picked the letter out of the box. As usual it was a single sheet of heavy cream vellum, with deckle-edges, folded in half. She spread the paper out. It was covered in neat, italic script. There were no mistakes, no deletions, no insertions. She knew that David had worked on it for a couple of days, before copying it out like some ancient illuminator of biblical texts. It was a script – her script – the distilled essence of his latest sexual imaginings. He would never have dared to ask her, face to face, to do the things the letter contained; she was sure of that. This was the way he had evolved of giving his fantasies full reign.

She read the page twice. Half of her – or was it more than half? – wished he would simply charge into the bedroom, throw her on the bed and take her without ceremony. The other half enjoyed the ritual dressing and preparation, and the peculiar sense of anticipation it gave her. She was not quite sure what inspired her excitement. Perhaps it was merely the fact that all this was so outré? Or was it the power, the element of control, the fact that David had cast her in the dominant role, master of his sexual pleasure? She had never played these sorts of games before and would certainly never have imagined that they would excite her. But, to her surprise, if she were honest with herself, she found they did. Which is why, she supposed, she had not only gone on seeing David Allston but had allowed the games to become increasingly more elaborate.

She heard David's footsteps climbing the stairs. The ten minutes were up. She knew he would have been counting the seconds. Quickly she swept the wrapping paper on to the floor and dimmed the lights to a pleasant glow. She placed the smaller, still unwrapped, box on the bedside table, then sat down on the edge of the bed again. As always she was quite surprised to find her pulse was racing.

He knocked on the door three times.

'Come,' she said.

The door opened. He was naked. His clothes would be neatly stacked on one of the sofas downstairs, his shoes lined up side by side, his shirt folded as though for a suitcase, even his socks rolled into coiled balls.

'Sh . . .' she murmured. 'Don't make a sound.' He closed the door behind him with infinite care, then turned towards her, his penis already beginning to stiffen. 'We have to be very quiet. No one must catch you in here with me. You know that, don't you?' It was the first line of the script. It invariably started in the same way.

'Yes,' he whispered. He stood with his back to the door, his eyes roaming her body.

'No one must ever find out about this. No one.' The second line was the same too.

'I know.'

'Come over here, then.'

He took a step forward then stopped, anticipating, like a bad actor, what the next line of the script would be.

'Stop. You know better than that, don't you?'

He looked shamefaced. His cock hardened further, growing to its full stature. 'Yes,' he said. He dropped to his knees on the long–pile cream carpet.

'That's better.'

Slowly he shuffled forward on his knees until he was right in front of her.

She raised her left foot and wriggled her nylon covered big toe against his left nipple. It made his cock quiver.

'You know what to do?' she said. Again this part of the script was always the same.

'Yes,' he whispered. Even if she hadn't been able to see the excited state of his cock, his expression would have betrayed how he felt. Sexual arousal blazed in his eyes, its tension etched in every line of his face. He took hold of her left foot with both hands and brought it up to his lips, kissing it lightly, little nibbling kisses all over the white nylon-covered flesh. He sucked gently on her toes, crowding them all into his mouth at the same time. A tear of fluid forced its way out of his glans.

'Now the other one,' she demanded, snatching her foot away and making him pick the other off the floor. He followed the same procedure.

Clare could not suppress a shudder of delight. She felt her excitement mounting. It was a

21

physical thing, a direct connection between the nerves in her toes and those in her sex. There was a certain thrill attached to having a man kneeling at her feet, prepared to do her bidding. But, of course, it wasn't really *her* bidding; it only appeared to be. What she was going to ask him to do was all the product of *his* imagination.

'All right, that's enough,' she said.

'It was lovely,' he whispered.

'You know what I want you to do now?' She stood up. Taking the back of his head in his hand, she pushed his face into her flat, pink silk-sheathed belly. She felt his hot breath against her flesh. Her sex throbbed. 'Do you know?'

'Yes,' he moaned, the word gagged by her body.

She released him. Very slowly he raised his hands to the white garter on her thigh and drew it down her leg. When he reached her ankle she raised her foot so he could pull it free. He immediately held the garter to his mouth, kissing the lace and inhaling the scent of her body. This was always the same too, an established part of the ritual.

'Get on with it,' she ordered.

David looped the garter around his wrist then crawled over to a large, bow-fronted chest of drawers with brass handles. He opened the bottom drawer and pulled out a pair of white satin French knickers with lace-trimmed legs. There were other things in the bottom drawer too, other props for his little dramas, but none would be used tonight.

'Don't make me,' he said pathetically, though it was clear it was what he wanted more desperately than anything else.

'You know it's what I want.' Another line from the script.

He got to his feet, stepped into the satin knickers and pulled them up over his legs. He had very slim, snake-like hips but even so the knickers were too tight. They stretched tautly over his navel, his phallus trapped inside them, every inch of it outlined under the satin. The tear of fluid it had produced immediately soaked into the material, darkening the white.

'Don't you look pretty?' Oddly enough it was true. There was something feminine about David's body. His skin was soft and very white and, although he had no muscle tone, he was not fat either. His only obvious display of masculinity pressed against the white satin.

'Please.'

'Come back here, now.'

He got back on to his knees. As he crawled back towards her she picked the small gold box from the bedside table and tore off the wrapping paper. Inside, as she'd guessed, was a black silk sleeping mask.

'If I screamed the whole house would come running.' That wasn't exactly what he'd written but it was close enough.

'Yes,' he said breathily, as he knelt with his hands on his knees in front of her once more.

'They'd see you like this.'

'Please don't scream.' He said it with conviction, completely engrossed in the imaginary situation.

'I won't. But only if you do exactly what I tell you to do.' Sometimes Clare wondered if the scenarios they acted out were based on fact. There had been many variations but the basic tenets were always the same: a man at the mercy of a woman. Had he smuggled himself into one of the maid's rooms at the country estate, in his adolescence perhaps, and been punished for his trouble in exactly this way? Would that explain his obsession, his burgeoning sexuality becoming fixated on a particularly strong experience?

The patch of wet on the front of the French knickers was getting larger and making the material transparent. She could actually see his glans and the eye of his penis from which the sticky fluid leaked.

'Well?' she said with all the imperiousness she could muster.

'Please, I'll do anything you say.'

'Put this on.' She threw the sleeping mask on to the floor in front of him. 'You don't think I'm going to let you see me naked, do you?'

'No.' He picked the mask up and slipped it over his eyes, adjusting the elasticated straps so that it fitted snugly.

Clare paused. She was very excited now. She found she had become wrapped up in his fantasy too. The sex she had had before meeting David had always been spontaneous, never knowing what would happen next. This was the other side of the coin, sex planned down to the last detail. She knew exactly what David was going to do to her next and she found that knowledge arousing.

She saw David's head moving very slightly, trying to pick up a sound as a clue to what she was doing. She found she was in the mood to tease him now, and kept perfectly still. Then, as quietly as she could, she extended her foot and pressed her toes against his cock. He started. That wasn't in the script.

'Is that nice?' She rubbed her foot up and down.

He didn't reply. He didn't say anything that he hadn't rehearsed.

'All right.' She reverted to her role. 'If you do as I say, no one will know you've been here. Is that understood?'

'Yes.'

'Good.' You know what you have to do now.' She stood up and held the back of his head again but this time maintained a distance from his face. His hands groped up between her legs, over the stocking tops to the top of her thighs. Pressing into the soft, hot flesh of her labia he struggled to locate the three poppers that held the gusset of the pink silk body in place.

His fingers fumbled around ineffectively, enjoying the liberty they had been allowed.

'Concentrate,' she scolded.

He pulled two of the poppers free but couldn't find the third. She stepped back, tutting loudly. 'Not very good.'

The third popper made a loud metallic click as she freed it. The two halves of the gusset parted, hanging down front and back. 'I hope you can do better than that.' The longer the game went on the easier she found it to play her role. What was more, the easier it came to her the more wrapped up in it she became. It *was* exciting. She could feel the impression his fingers had made on her sex.

Clare sat on the bed. She put her foot up on to his chest for the second time. 'Kiss it,' she said almost in a whisper. she wondered if, years ago, David *had* tried to take advantage of one of the maids and she, seeing an opportunity to blackmail the young master, threatening to go to his father, had used him as shamelessly as this. If she were an actress she'd certainly use that scenario to provide her motivation.

David brought her foot up to his mouth and kissed it again. This time he kissed the inside of her ankle and immediately began to work his mouth up her calf. When he got to her knee she ordered him to stop. Resting her heel on his shoulder she raised her other foot, this time pushing her toes against his lips. 'Now the other one,' she said.

He repeated the process, kissing and nibbling his way up along the white nylon. She rested this heel against his other shoulder, spreading her knees apart and allowing his mouth to venture up to her thigh. She flicked the gusset of the body up. Had he not been blindfold he would have had a perfect view of her sex.

His tongue licked at her stocking top. As he leant forward she rocked back until she was laying on the bed. She hooked her legs around his neck and crossed her ankles, splaying her thighs further apart, her sex open for him.

She could feel her body pulsing rhythmically, playing its own sensual music. Her hips were undulating almost unconsciously, as David's mouth worked its way over the nylon welt and on to the creamy soft flesh above it. She was naturally olive skinned and the contrast between the very white welt of the stocking and her skin was marked. After the coarseness of the nylon against his tongue and lips it would also seem impossibly soft.

He licked his way right up to her labia, moaning with pleasure as his mouth made its first contact with her sex.

'You naughty boy.' There wasn't much left of the script now. 'You are very naughty, aren't you?'

'Oh yes.' He formed the word without taking his mouth away from her. She could feel his lips moving.

'I shouldn't allow you to do this, should I?'

She found herself imagining she was in some dingy below-stairs room in the Allstons' country estate, forcing the young master to give her pleasure. The maid would have been a first-class bitch requiring his attentions night after night, constantly reminding him that refusal would mean reporting him to his tyrannical father.

Clare could feel her sex was wet. With her labia spread open by the position of her legs, her clitoris was exposed and she could feel it throbbing.

'No, no, you shouldn't,' he said.

'But I'm going to.'

As she said this his tongue pressed against her clitoris. He was good at this. Very good. No man had ever been better in her experience. His mouth seemed able to mould itself to her sex. He had a way of stretching her labia with his lips, pulling her clitoris taut while, at the same time, his tongue worked on it with the most perfect of touches, alternating between stroking it up and down, pushing it back against the pubic bone, or tapping it at its most sensitive spot.

It all made her writhe with pleasure. She dug her heels into his back, levering her sex still harder against his mouth, and snapping her head over to one side as this produced a new jolt of intense feeling. His chin was jutting against the opening of her vagina. The wetness of her sex was seeping all over it.

She knew what he would do next. For her, at

27

least, the fantasy was slipping away, as waves of physical pleasure unleashed their hold on her. The way his tongue seemed to be able to create piercing shards of intense pleasure astonished her. Now she didn't need anything else; mind games were simply surplus to requirements. The only thing she needed was what he was already supplying, altering the position of his mouth slightly, angling it up to make the opening of her vagina accessible so he could slip one, then two, then three fingers into it. He did not penetrate her with them. He held them there, waiting for the right moment, the blindfold concentrating all his attention on his sense of touch. He would feel when she was ready, when the provocation of his tongue on her clitoris took her right to the edge.

She was rigid now, the muscles of her legs looped around his neck corded and hard, her fingers clutching at the sheet as if for extra support. 'Yes,' she moaned.

At that second she came. The flood of her orgasm drowned her in sensation, but not before he'd driven his fingers up into her sex, as deep as they would possibly go, the impact of one chasing the impact of the other. Feeling was layered upon feeling. The wave of orgasm was extended, deepened, honed to a new intensity. Clare gasped, still able to feel, in the middle of this maelstrom of sensation, the relentless movement of his tongue against her clitoris, each tiny stroke magnified and amplified into a whole new panoply of pleasure.

It must have eventually ended. He sensed her crisis pass and pulled his fingers gently out of her body, moving back on his haunches as she raised her legs from his shoulders.

It always ended the same way, at least it had since she'd agreed to co-operate with the ritual. He remained where he was kneeling in front of her, still blindfolded, his back straight, his hands at his sides. She would roll off the bed and walk over to the bedside table, her stockings rasping against each other as she moved. There was a bottle of perfume in the top drawer of the bedside table – cheap, flowery perfume. She'd take it out of the drawer and carry it back to where he knelt. Sitting on the bed again, she'd take the stopper out of the bottle and rub it under his nose. He would inhale deeply and moan.

Lifting her foot, she'd rub her sole against his distended phallus. Instantly she'd feel it jerk. Equally quickly the white satin would darken and the already wet patch enlarge to cover most of the front of the knickers, his body shuddering profoundly as it did so, like a ship holed below the waterline. He'd drop forward, his head against her knee, clutching her leg in his arms.

It was always the same. It was almost five months since Clare had had penetrative sex.

# Chapter Two

*HAD SHE KNOWN* Bridget Goldsmith planned to descend on London, Clare would never have allowed work to start on the extension. What with all the necessary planning and work the visit entailed, the last thing she needed was to come home at night to a house that looked as though it were in the process of being demolished.

She could have moved out. She could have gone to stay with her friend Angela. Instead, once the builders had breached the back wall, she had moved her clothes and make-up into the front bedroom, next to the bathroom, and she had made do, eating out, since her kitchen had disappeared, and taking comfort from the fact that George Wickes assured her the building work would definitely be finished in two weeks' time.

There were, however, two compensations. The first was that she could see the work in progress and check it was all going to plan. It only took two days to knock out the wall to which the extension would be fitted and after that every day brought new additions, the new walls rising, floors and ceilings gradually fitted in place. She began to be able to imagine what it would look like when it was finished.

The other compensation was more venal: Gary. Clare had asked him what his surname was. Newby, Gary Newby. He maintained his pattern of being the first to arrive and the last to leave. He frequently worked stripped to his shorts. Although she was not able to observe him as closely as she had from the back bedroom, she still caught glimpses of that magnificent body.

Exactly one week before Bridget's arrival Clare had taken a call from Angela, her oldest friend, just as she'd arrived home from work.

'Hi, darling, how's tricks?' Angela always sounded chipper.

'Don't ask. I'm up to my eyes in building rubble.'

'That's what I thought. Do you fancy a bite to eat and . . .'

'And?'

'A little diversion.' Angela Barker was a journalist for a glossy magazine, a sinewy blonde whose long hair seemed to attract men like moths to a flame. Like moths too, many had got themselves badly burned. Angela was forthright and down-to-earth and not one to suffer fools, even handsome or rich fools, gladly. Her attitude to men was entirely pragmatic. If they gave her what she wanted at the time they were tolerated. If not they were abandoned.

'OK. How long?'

'Ten minutes.' Angela lived in a mansion-block just around the corner.

'Fifteen. I've got to change.'

'Done.'

Replacing the phone under the dust-sheet that

covered the table in the sitting room, Clare rushed upstairs. It was always the same with Angela. Everything was arranged at the last minute. Nothing was ever planned.

She managed to shower and change into a summer frock in ten minutes, seeing Angela's Ford Escort Cabriolet draw up outside as she applied her make-up.

The doorbell rang, but, before she could get downstairs, Gary, who was clearing up after the day's work and taking two bucket-fulls of rubbish to the skip, had answered it for her.

'Hi,' Angela said, none too subtly eyeing the bulging muscles of Gary's naked chest. 'God, Clare you really should stop taking the HRT,' she added, laughing.

'I'm Gary,' the builder said self-consciously. 'Just got to drop these in the skip.'

'You can drop me in the skip anytime,' Angela retorted, as Clare rushed downstairs.

'Excuse my friend, Gary; she's a wolf in wolf's clothing.'

'Yeah,' he smiled, heading out to the skip.

'He's gorgeous,' Angela said. The women kissed on both cheeks.

'Got time to see what used to be my house?'

Clare led the way to the back of the house, where a gaping hole was supported by a new RSJ.

'Oh, it's lovely,' Angela joked. 'Did you do this?'

Gary had come back in, carrying the empty buckets. 'Some of it.'

'How much longer?' Angela asked.

'Not long now.'

'Two weeks? Looks like it's going to take months.'

'Naw,' Gary said seriously. 'The basic struc-ture's in.'

'Gary Newby, this is Angela Barker.' Clare intro-duced them.

'Pleased to meet you,' he said. 'Won't shake hands. They're filthy.'

'You are a big boy, aren't you?' Angela comment-ed, unabashed.

'Angela, behave!'

'Such big strong muscles. I like a bit of rough trade.'

'That's enough, Angela. Come on, let's go. You have to excuse my friend, she has a mission to be outrageous.'

'That's all right with me,' Gary said. Angela was wearing a tight one-piece suit in cream, its low-cut neckline showing a great deal of her ample cleav-age and the material clung tightly to her long legs. In the roving eye department Gary and Angela were evenly matched.

'Can you lock up, Gary?'

'No problem. Have a good time.'

Clare pulled Angela into the hall. She opened the front door and bundled her out, but not before Angela had said, in her loudest voice, 'What a hunk!'

She repeated it as they climbed into the car. 'Now I know why you wouldn't move in with me,' she added.

'I hardly noticed him,' Clare lied airily.

'And?' Angela started the engine and drove away, seemingly at a hundred miles an hour.

'And what?'

'Do I have to spell it out?'

Clare rapidly did up her safety-belt as they cornered with a screech of tyres.

'Oh, come on, Angela – he's a builder.'

'You're not a snob, are you?'

'I don't mean that. I can hardly seduce him though, can I? What am I supposed to do, drift down to the concrete mixer in my black negligée? Anyway, he's probably married with four children.'

'Still . . .' Angela let the word linger in the air. 'So talking of sex, how's David?'

'The same as ever. Just the same.'

'What does that mean?'

Clare had not shared the secret of David's complex sex-life. 'Oh, I suppose I should end it really. It's not going anywhere.'

'Why? I thought you liked him.'

'I do. But "like" isn't "love".'

'Oh, keep him on the hook until you get a better offer. That's what I'd do. Don't burn your boats.'

'Oh, it's difficult.'

'Is he good in bed?' Angela always got to the point.

'So-so.'

'Ah.' Angela sounded as though she had just discovered the meaning of life. 'Drop him then.'

'A few seconds ago you told me to keep him until someone better comes along.'

'Yes, but if he's no good in the sack there's no point.'

'I've got to do something.'

'There's always Gary.' Angela grinned. She had a large, sensual mouth and a set of very white teeth.

'And what about your sex-life?' Clare asked, glad to change the subject.

Since Angela's propensity to consume men at

an alarming rate was an inexhaustible topic, her tales of her latest adventures took them through the rest of the journey.

They fetched up in Streatham. Angela parked the car and headed for an old-fashioned-looking pub on a busy corner of a main road.

'I thought we were going to eat,' Clare complained, quite hungry now.

'I've got to just do this first. Come on, it starts in five minutes.'

The poster outside the pub was life-sized. It featured an incredibly muscular black man, with a deep barrel chest, and large prominent veins on all his bulging muscles. His head was shaved and his body oiled, the leather pouch that covered his genitals almost grotesquely distended. Mr Macho, according to the poster, was performing tonight, at seven, nine and ten thirty.

'Oh no,' Clare said, when she realised what Mr Macho was likely to be doing. 'I'm not going in there.'

'Why not?'

'He's a male stripper, right?'

'I've got to write about it for the magazine.'

'It'll be obscene.'

'Oh come on, don't be so po-faced.'

Angela pushed through the panelled glass doors, their brass handles and fingerplates brightly polished. Inside, the ground floor was packed with people, mostly women. Angela produced two free passes and flashed them at the large bouncer who guarded the stairs to the upstairs room where the performance would take place. He grunted and allowed them to push past the hordes of other women who were buying tickets at the table to his left, which had been hastily arranged to act as an impromptu box office. The women all chatted and giggled and nudged each other with nervous excitement.

Angela led the way upstairs. They found themselves in a large rectangular room with a circular rostrum at one end. The room was already packed exclusively with women. They ferried drinks from a long bar on one wall to the tables, tin trays laden with gin and tonics and pint glasses of lager, most of the tables exhibiting an array of examples of what had been previously consumed.

The nervous excitement of the women was more pronounced up here; the heat, the alcohol and the level of noise increasing the women's volubility, which, in turn, was an indication that a certain amount of bravado was necessary to get them through the evening.

Clare looked around. She guessed that few of the women had ever been to such an event before. Some, despite the drink and eager comments, looked distinctly uncomfortable. Or perhaps that was just her, reading her own feelings into their blank faces. She most certainly didn't want to be there, and would have turned round and left but for the fact she knew that for the next ten years Angela would have ragged her for her lack of daring.

Clare searched for a place to hide and pulled her friend over to the far end of the bar, the furthest point from the rostrum.

'Do you want a drink?' Angela shouted over the noise.

'Not really.'

There were four large Bose speakers suspended from the ceiling in each corner of the room. Suddenly they produced a loud tapping noise, followed by the ear-splitting wail of feedback, as a woman in a man's black dinner jacket and bow-tie dragged a microphone on its stand into the centre of the rostrum. The spotlights suspended on a bar above the stage were faded up, lighting the whole area in a rose-tinted hue.

'Ladies . . .' the announcer said, as soon as the whine in the sound system was sorted out. 'Ladies, this is what you've all been waiting for.' There were cries of 'Yes, yes, yes,' from the audience. 'The Freeman's Arms,' the woman continued, 'is proud to present for your entertainment tonight, the one and only, the exciting, the dynamic, Mr Macho!'

The scream of approval was deafening. High-heel shoes stomped on the wooden floor as the lights in the room dimmed.

A silver lurex curtain had been hung on the wall at the back of the rostrum. The curtain twitched. It twitched again; then, obscenely, tented outwards, something poking it from the other side just below waist level. The women roared at the size of the protrusion.

'Oh, god,' Clare muttered, glaring at Angela.

'Not exactly subtle,' she conceded. She had taken a spiral bound notebook from her handbag and was writing notes in shorthand.

The curtain was thrown aside and a tall black man stalked on to the stage. He was wearing chiffon harem pantaloons over tight, red, satin briefs. His chest was hairless and just as muscular as the photograph outside had suggested. As he stepped forward the loudspeakers began to play an instrumental version of 'Goldfinger'. In his hand Mr Macho held a black rod, a larger version of a magician's wand.

'Did you think that was me?' he yelled into the microphone. He addressed the question to the women sitting nearest to the rostrum.

'Yes,' the audience screamed as one.

'Naughty girls! I'm *much* bigger than that.'

He tossed the wand to the woman in the dinner suit, who had retired to the side of the curtain, then began gyrating his hips in time to the music.

'Look at those muscles,' Angela shouted into Clare's ear. 'Reminds me of your Gary.'

They reminded Clare of Gary too, and, despite herself, she felt a pang of desire.

The stripper began to pull the chiffon pantaloons down over his hips, turning his back to the audience and bending over so they were peeled over his very tight buttocks. When he got them to his knees he jumped around to face the audience again. He sat on the floor, jack-knifed his legs out in front of him and pulled the pantaloons off over his ankles.

'Now it gets interesting,' he promised as he sprang to his feet.

'I really don't want to see any more,' Clare murmured.

'Don't you, love?' asked the woman standing next to her at the bar. 'I do. I want to see the whole bloody thing.'

Very slowly, constantly grinding his hips in time to the music, the black man hooked his thumbs into the waistband of the satin briefs and pulled them down an inch or two, then coyly pulled them up again to cries of 'More!' from the crowd. After repeating this teasing three or four times he finally stripped the satin to where it was just covering his genitals. He turned around again and quickly pulled the briefs to the floor, his tight buttocks dimpled at the side.

The women screamed out obscene remarks as to what they wanted him to do next. He smiled at them over his shoulder and tutted into the microphone. Then he spun round a complete 360 degrees, so fast none of the women glimpsed a thing. He did this twice more, before turning slowly so he faced the audience. His genitals were covered in a black leather pouch, held in place by a draw-string. It looked as though he was partially erect under the leather.

'Now I need a volunteer,' he said. Immediately he leapt off the rostrum into the crowd. A follow-spot had been switched on and tracked him as he sat squarely on the lap of a large, very overweight woman in a bright orange dress, his hand groping one of her massive breasts. The woman blushed a deep red but put her arms around the man and hugged him tightly. He had a struggle to escape from her clutches.

When he finally managed it, he ran amongst the tables up to the bar, where a young brunette in a very short black mini-dress was standing with a drink in her hand. He took the drink from her, tasted it and grimaced. 'Her horse has got diabetes,' he joked. 'Do you want to help me out?' he asked her, taking her hand.

'No way,' she responded, snatching her hand away.

He bound over to a pretty blonde in a black halter top, white hot pants and black tights. She backed away but her friends pushed her towards him.

'We have a volunteer,' he announced, taking the girl by the arm and leading her to the rostrum, her resistance only nominal.

As they climbed on to the stage there was wild applause and cries of 'Get it off'. The music had changed to a slow version of 'Man with the Golden Gun'.

'On your knees,' the stripper ordered the girl, grinding his hips to the music again.

The blonde giggled, looked to her friends for encouragement and then, egged on by them, got down on one knee.

'Right, here we go, ladies!' He pulled the girl's hand up to the draw-string at the front of the pouch. She did not hesitate. She pulled the bow that held it in place and tore the black leather pouch away, holding it aloft like a hunter's trophy to an enormous cheer from the audience.

'Can we go now?' Clare wondered. Angela ignored her, straining to see the black man's cock.

The stripper dropped to his knees. He pushed the blonde back on the rostrum and climbed on top of her. He bucked his hips up and down as if he were having sex with her, while she, in turn, folded her black, nylon-sheathed legs over his back. The women in the audience began to chant in time to the man's thrusts. 'In!' they screamed, followed by, 'Out!'

For the first time, and very much to her surprise, the spectacle affected Clare. She felt a throb of excitement. She could not tear her eyes away from the big, powerful muscles of the man's buttocks and thighs, which rippled as he powered forward. Her excitement flowed from unbidden thoughts about what it would feel like to have that broad, hard body on top of her, thrusting an equally broad and hard cock into the depths of her meltingly soft sex. The surge of feeling made her realise what she'd been missing all these months.

The black man peeled the girl's legs from around his back and sprung to his feet, his cock slapping against his thigh.

'Who's next?' he bellowed, leaping into the audience again. He picked up a tumbler containing a gin and tonic, dipped his cock into it and stirred it around. 'Cocktails, anyone?' he teased.

'Let's go,' Clare said. This time she wasn't going to take no for an answer. She took Angela by the arm and began pushing her way through the crowd.

Unfortunately the stripper spotted the movement. He leapt through the tables and planted himself squarely in front of her, his muscular frame glistening under the light from the follow-spot. 'Not leaving already?' he said. 'Can I mix you a drink?' He indicated his cock.

'No, thank you,' Clare replied. Even through the baying cries of the women he must have been able to tell from the tone of her voice that she was serious. Or perhaps it was the expression on her face. In any event his experience told him she was not the right woman to use in his act. But he was getting an entirely different reaction from Angela, who was at Clare's shoulder.

Dancing up to her, he grabbed Angela's hand. She squealed with delight and surprise as he pulled her towards him and began wriggling his body against her like a snake.

It was only a matter of seconds before he'd transferred his attention to another woman, sitting at the nearest table. He pulled her chair out to face him and straddled her knees, without sitting on them, so his cock was right in front of her face.

Clare didn't wait to see any more. She wrestled

her way to the exit and down the stairs, Angela
following in her wake. Pushing through the
double doors she stood on the busy street outside.

'Well, that was fun,' Angela said as she joined
her. 'What a mover!'

'You didn't really enjoy it?'

'Come on, let's go and eat. I'm starving.' They
walked back to the car. 'All right, I admit it wasn't
sexy. But it was interesting. And that guy had a
beautiful body. Have you ever had a guy like that?'

'No.'

'Don't you wonder what it would be like?'

Clare had wondered what it would be like with
Gary. 'No.'

'I think it would be great.'

'Is that a fantasy of yours? Some hunk?'

'Yes, a nice bit of rough trade,' Angela said,
unlocking the car. 'Isn't that what we'd all like,
really?'

Clare didn't answer that question.


'You're sure you don't mind?'

'Why should I mind? If it gets the job done more
quickly it's good, isn't it? The sooner I get out of
this mess the better.'

'I don't want to mess up your evening.'

'What evening? I'm only going to watch telly.'

'All right then. I'll only be another hour.'

Gary, as usual, had been the only man left
working when she got back from work. He'd asked
Clare if she'd mind him working late, to finish the
last section of plaster on the new interior walls.

'Do you want a beer?' she enquired.

'Can I have it when I'm done?'

'Of course.'

Clare wandered up to the front bedroom. As that

and the bathroom were the only places not affected by dust and rubble she'd put her telly at the foot of the bed. She switched it on and lay on the bed watching it without being conscious of what was actually on. She had had another hard day preparing for Bridget's visit, due in three days' time. Most of the presentation was ready but Clare had found mistakes in some of the statistics and had ordered last-minute changes to the marketing strategy. Although each country was going to be given the same packaging and artwork, Clare wanted it made clear by the advertising agency that the individual ads should be tailor-made for each national campaign. Results of product-launches in which an American commercial had merely been re-voiced and run without any other change had been extremely disappointing, though she knew that that was the approach Bridget Goldsmith favoured. She wanted the presentation to contain the evidence that supported her own point of view.

The sun had been out all day and as the house faced south – another reason Clare slept in the back – the front bedroom was hot. The sultry heat made her drowsy but the loud thuds and bangs as Gary worked away prevented her from dozing off.

Instead she daydreamed. Gary was stripped to his shorts again. Inevitably she compared his physique to that of the black stripper. Perhaps the black man's muscles were slightly better defined, the result, no doubt, of pumping iron in a gym. Gary's muscles were formed by hard physical labour.

Like most women, she thought, Clare had always believed a man's mind was more important than his body, but she could not deny that she had been acutely aroused by watching the black man performing simulated intercourse. Equally Gary's body was affecting her. Over the last weeks she had been intensely aware of it.

She wondered what Gary would do if she wandered downstairs in something light and flimsy. The collection of lingerie donated by David Allston was quite extensive. She could put on the pink silk body. Or there was a short, black, lace slip with spaghetti straps, the lace making it almost totally transparent. What would he do if she wafted into the rubble of the back room wearing that?

Clare was not naive about sex. She had pursued everything in her life with tenacity, determination and thirst for knowledge. This attitude had served her well in business. She had risen rapidly through the ranks of KissCo and was the youngest managing director of any equivalent company in the UK. It had served her well in her sex life too. She had pursued her sexual aims with quite as much ambition as her career. She had selected lovers on the basis of merit, quickly discarding men who proved unsatisfactory lovers. Some might have thought her ruthless but Clare liked sex and saw no point wasting time in a relationship where, at the end of the day, it was going to leave her unfulfilled.

Her thirst for knowledge had made her a formidable competitor in business. She knew more about almost everything in the cosmetics industry than any of her rivals. She knew more about how business worked too, about financing, sales promotion and advertising, and the psychology of management. There wasn't a single aspect of KissCo's operation she did not understand better than the departmental head who ran it.

She had applied the same zeal to her private life. She had become interested in art deco and had researched it to such an extent that she was regarded by some auction houses as an expert on the period. Her enjoyment of sex had motivated her to approach that subject with similar application. She had bought books, watched porno movies, and talked to all her friends about their experiences. She had been astonished, but not shocked, by the diversity of sexual behaviour. Over the years she had read about every sort of sexual perversion. They fascinated her. Not because she had the slightest desire to be tied to a mediaeval rack and whipped, or dress from head to toe in black rubber, or any of the hundred-and-one other activities the books graphically described, but because it never ceased to amaze her that such things could be sexually arousing at all.

But quest for knowledge had revealed more practical information. She had, for instance, become an expert on masturbation. In school the basic sex lessons had barely touched on more egocentric goals, but her extra-curricular reading, at that time confined to various how-to-do-what books, had explained in great detail the advantages and techniques involved. She had quickly learned to explore her own body with the same thoroughness she employed on everything else. Later, having successfully invented a series of procedures to stimulate herself to very vivid orgasms, a friend had told her about dildos. Their introduction into her masturbation routine had been nothing short of explosive, the combination of a hard cylindrical object buried in her vagina and the artful cajoling of her clitoris producing enviable results.

Her knowledge of the byways of sexual experience had been good preparation for David Allston. She found him attentive and charming and, what was more important, the way he manipulated her body, the way he used his fingers and mouth on her, had given her intense pleasure, even if when it came to full sexual intercourse things had been less than satisfactory. Had he not been so good at foreplay, he would have become a victim of her ruthless selection policy, the survival of the fittest. But he was good: foreplay had become the main event.

When after their first few weeks together he'd brought her a gift-wrapped, black lace teddy and a pair of black hold-up stockings, with lace tops, and a little card suggesting that she might like to go and change into them while he waited downstairs, she'd found the idea exciting. There was something about getting dressed up for sex that appealed to her. Her response had clearly encouraged David. The gifts had become more elaborate, the cards extended into letters, his brief attempts at intercourse abandoned in favour of more exotic gratification.

Since the rituals had always resulted in a wonderfully satisfying orgasm for Clare, she had raised no objections. There was no one else in her life at that moment. But recently the rituals had become ritualised. She began to yearn for spontaneity. As her reaction to the black stripper had clearly demonstrated, she yearned for penetration too.

Clare felt a strong and powerful pulse emanating from her sex. It caused her nipples to pucker. They felt cold, little chips of marble nestling in her bra.

Getting up off the bed, she switched off the television. She usually had a bath or shower when she got home but had decided to wait until Gary had finished. She supposed she felt faintly embarrassed about being naked while he was in the house, however silly that seemed.

Clare thought of herself as liberated and independently minded. She wasn't too concerned with social niceties or the quibbles and taboos of conventional morality. That did not mean, unfortunately, she thought, that she had escaped the conventions of the sexual role that she had been nurtured in from an earlier age. In the mood she was in she would have loved to be able to go downstairs, not fancifully dressed in flimsy lingerie like something from a scene in a porno film, but dressed as she was now, and ask Gary if he would like to go to bed with her. As simple as that. But it was just not possible. She couldn't do it. Man *had* to proposition woman. Those were the rules. As yet female liberation had not changed much in that direction. At least, not for her. She'd seen Angela Barker take the initiative in a way she would never have had the courage to do.

'Mrs Markham?' Gary's voice interrupted her reverie.

'Yes?' She stepped out of her bedroom. He was standing at the bottom of the stairs.

'All done. It didn't take as long as I thought.' He was pulling a check shirt on over his chest.

'Do you want that beer now?' she asked, walking downstairs. He was looking up at her, with a serious expression on his face.

'Thanks,' he said.

She went to the fridge. The old kitchen had been demolished and the fridge stood on a wall in the dining room, covered in a film of dust. She took a beer. The glasses had been packed away but Gary usually drank straight from the bottle. She managed to find a bottle opener and peeled off the metal top. Still feeling coquettish she wondered if she was actually going to do anything other than give him a beer.

'Aren't you going to have one?' he wondered, walking back into the dining room and taking the bottle from her.

'I'm fine,' she said.

'See.' He indicated the new wall which now formed the back of the house. 'Plastered all that up.' Pink plaster covered the whole of the area where the new kitchen would be. 'I'm not in tomorrow. Got to let the chippies in to lay the floors and put in the skirting boards.'

'Mr Wickes said you'd be finished next week.'

'Yeah, definite.'

'It was quick.' He was handsome. She loved the way his lips curled up at the edges as he talked. She loved his rugged, tanned hands, and the way his blue eyes seemed to sparkle. He had the air of a man who had discovered the meaning of life and found it permanently amusing.

'Got to keep the customer happy.'

'Don't you want to sit down?' Three of her oldest straight-backed chairs had been ranged against the dining-room wall and covered with dust sheets for the use of the workmen. 'You've been on your feet all day.'

'Must be going,' he said.

'Not another beer?' The first had been consumed rapidly.

'Yeah. OK. One more. Thanks.'

He sat on one of the chairs as she took another beer from the fridge and opened it. She wondered what she thought she was doing. Why on earth hadn't she just let him leave?

'Cheers,' he said.

'Have you worked for Mr Wickes long?' She sat down on the chair at the end of the row, leaving one between them.

'Five years. He's a good man. Looks after his men.'

'Is that what you always wanted to be, a builder?'

'Me? No. I wanted to be an astronaut. I wanted to be the first man to walk on the far side of the moon. I'd have liked to stand there looking out into space and not be able to see the earth.'

Clare saw the idea create a spark in his eyes. For some reason that made her heart go out to him. 'Why didn't you?' She leant forward, resting her elbows on her knees.

'What, with a CSE in woodwork? No chance.'

Clare felt confused and uncomfortable and hot. She wasn't seriously going to try and seduce him, was she? That was just an idle daydream. She thought of Angela's reference to 'rough trade'. She wondered what her friend would do in this situation.

'Are you married?' The question came out all wrong. It sounded too blunt and obvious. 'I'm sorry, none of my business.' That made it worse. She felt herself blushing.

'No, never have been either,' he said, appearing not to notice her embarrassment.

'Involved?' She could hardly believe she'd said that.

'No. Look, I'd better go.'

'There's no hurry, is there?' She smiled, a tiny rather nervous smile, and leant back in her chair trying to imagine she was Angela, cool, determined and fearless.

'Look, Mrs Markham . . .'

'Ms. I'm not married. Like you, I never have been.'

'I think I should tell you something.'

'And that is?'

He looked directly into her eyes for the first time. She felt her heart pumping faster. 'I've been hanging around here a lot.'

'Have you?'

'You know I have. It's because you're a fantastic-looking bird.'

With blinding clarity, like the sun coming out from behind heavy cloud, Clare suddenly knew what she was going to do. 'Does this happen a lot, then?' she asked.

'What?'

'Women you're working for, throwing themselves at you.'

He laughed. It was a lovely open sound. 'And here was me thinking I was doing the throwing . . . And, yeah, as it happens, it does. Practically every house I'm in some bird is all over me like a rash. It's a wonder I get any work done.' He said it with self-depreciating humour that Clare found irresistible.

'You *are* a very attractive man.'

'I'm glad you think so.'

'Are you?'

'If you want the truth, Ms Markham, I've really

been lusting after you.'

Clare smiled. Ten minutes ago she would have been alarmed if he had said such a thing. Now it pleased her. 'Lusting isn't really the right word, is it?' She was conscious that her cultivated received pronunciation sounded artificial against his earthy, South London vowels.

'Why not?'

'Because lusting implies urgency and force.'

He laughed that gorgeous laugh again. 'I could have been arrested for doing what I've been thinking.'

'And now?' Clare asked. She couldn't remember ever having been so bold.

'Is this a wind-up? Are you serious?'

She didn't need to think about her answer. Being so daring was turning her on. He was turning her on. 'Perfectly,' she said in her precise, clipped accent.

He put the bottle down on the floor with studied concentration, then slowly got to his feet. He stood directly in front of her, looking down into her eyes, his expression quizzical. Then he stooped, put one arm around her shoulders and one under her knees and, with no apparent effort, lifted her up, cradling her like a baby. He brought his lips to hers and kissed her hard, his tongue plunging into her mouth, hot and phallus-like.

Clare felt a pulse of desire so strong it made her whole body shudder. Suspended in his arms she felt almost weightless, and for some reason that gave her a sense of vulnerability. But the vulnerability was exciting. She couldn't ever remember a man picking her up physically before, nor any with the strength to do so. She kissed Gary back hard, wrapping her arms around his neck and grinding her mouth against his, enjoying the huge sense of exhilaration that shot through her. It wiped away any doubts she had about what she was doing.

'I need a shower,' he said, finally breaking the kiss.

'Upstairs,' she said breathlessly. He smelt of sweat. At any other time she might have found the smell unpleasant. At this moment it was intoxicating.

Without putting her down, he walked out into the hall and climbed the stairs. He knew where the bathroom was and pushed the door open with his foot.

'Don't put me down yet,' she said, as she felt him stoop to release her.

'Why not?'

'I like it. You're so strong.'

'I have to be,' he said, grinning. 'And you're so soft. You smell like flowers.' He kissed her again, lightly this time, using his tongue to trace the outline of her lips. He kissed her cheeks and her forehead and her nose. He kissed her eyelids, then her mouth again, but this time as forcefully as he had downstairs.

Clare was melting with passion. Her body seemed to have turned liquid, as liquid as the juices she knew were oozing out of her sex. She had never had sex with a man she had known for such a short period of time. She had never had sex without carefully vetting the man first and considering all the consequences and repercussions. The fact that fifteen minutes ago Gary Newby was someone with whom she'd exchanged no more than casual small talk made her feel almost light-headed with arousal. Hadn't she longed for spontaneity?

'Let me shower,' he insisted, putting her down. 'I'm dirty. Plaster-dust all over.' A large bulge pushed out the fly of his sawn-off jeans. He stripped off his shirt.

'You're a very sexy man, aren't you?' Clare purred. Though her feet were back on the floor she felt as if she were floating.

She ran her hand over the denim and unzipped his flies. 'God, I feel so naughty.' As if to demonstrate, she fished inside the jeans. He was wearing white boxer shorts. She fought her way inside them until her fingers closed on his hot, hard penis. 'That's what I want,' she said, pulling it out.

His cock was large, long, thick and circumcised, the diameter of the glans slightly bigger than the shaft that supported it. The ridge at the bottom of the glans was also very pronounced like a miniature ski-jump.

Gary unbuckled his belt and pulled his jeans down with the boxer shorts. His cock was still caught in the fly of the shorts and was dragged down with them, until it suddenly sprung free, quivering and vibrant, a proud totem to his masculinity. 'Let me shower,' he repeated, pulling off his heavy steel-capped boots and his socks so he could strip his jeans and shorts over his ankles.

What Clare actually wanted was for him to take her there and then. She wanted to be screwed. She wanted to be fucked. The words excited her. She was trying to think of a single reason why she couldn't have what she wanted.

Gary reached for the mixer taps and turned the water on. He climbed into the bath and let the water flow over him. He reached for the soap and lathered his body, then allowed the water to wash the lather away. The water ran pink with the plaster dust. It took a matter of seconds but to Clare it seemed like hours.

'No,' she said as he reached for a towel, not prepared to wait any longer. 'I want you like this.'

Without waiting for him to respond she grabbed the edge of the bath with both hands, bent over, straightened her back and wriggled her bottom from side to side, hoping he would take the hint.

He did. With water still dripping from his body, he climbed out of the bath and stood behind her. 'You can't wait, can you,' he said, stating the obvious.

'No, I can't. I've had to wait too long already. For heaven's sake, Gary . . .' She looked up at him, letting him see the need in her eyes, '. . . can't you see what you've done to me?' As if to illustrate the point she pulled the light cotton shirt-waister she was wearing up over her hips. With a total lack of modesty she had never exhibited before, she drew the gusset of her silky white panties to one side and thrust her buttocks up towards him. She knew he would be able to see her sex. It would be glistening with wetness.

'Look at that,' he breathed, momentarily hypnotised by the spectacle.

'Gary,' she whined. Voyeurism was not the point of this exercise.

'Yeah. Right,' he said. Gary thought of himself as experienced with women, but this woman was something new. Her cut-glass accent and the air of confidence and sophistication she exuded had attracted him to her from the start. But she wasn't like any of the girls he dated, and he'd never imagined he'd even get to first base. Women like her, rungs above him on the social ladder, simply didn't get involved with brickies, even brickies who did plastering too, even brickies with blonde hair and blue, come-to-bed eyes. Even the single women whose houses he'd worked on, if they were educated and posh like Clare Markham, had never displayed anything but cursory politeness. Oh, he wasn't naive enough to believe they didn't stare at his body and wonder. But looking wasn't doing. Until now.

He moved up behind Clare, gripped the top of her hips, and forced his erection into the cleft of her buttocks. He found her blatancy exciting.

'*Yes*,' she hissed. She hadn't had a man inside her for five months. She hadn't realised how much tension that had caused until it was about to be released.

He bucked his hips and guided his cock into the crease of her labia. He could feel her heat and wetness.

'Yes,' she repeated. 'I need it.' She squirmed her buttocks from side to side, feeling his glans knocking against them. She felt his cock nestling into the opening of her vagina which seemed to purse around it, welcoming it with a kiss.

He waited, his fingers gripping like a vice. She tried to push back at him but his hold was too tight. He was teasing her, making her wait. It only increased her arousal. At that moment she could have sworn she had never wanted a man more in her life, that she had never been so totally and absolutely consumed by lust. Nothing else mattered but the moment he chose to plunge inside her. She could feel the length of her vagina contracting, like a mouth desperate for air. The seconds stretched into hours. She actually believed she would come like this, come over the crown of his cock without further penetration, if he didn't do something soon.

But that proposition was not put to the test. Without any warning Gary bucked his hips and lunged his cock forward. It drove up into her, parting the soft, silky wet walls of her vagina, stretching her, filling her more completely than she had ever been filled before. He did not withdraw it again. Instead, while his hands pulled her back on him, using his considerable strength to flatten her buttocks against his iron hard navel, he pushed even deeper. It was only a matter of a fraction of an inch but it felt like he had broken through some barrier in her body, some secret barrier she had not known about, another hymen buried so deep only his size had managed to breach it.

And that was enough. Enough to produce a surge of feeling that blossomed instantly into an orgasm, an orgasm that consumed her like the flames of a fire consumed oxygen. It affected every part of her, made her tremble uncontrollably, made every muscle contract, every sinew stretch, her body completely embroiled in it. She thought she could hear herself screaming the word 'god' over and over again but whether she had actually pronounced it or whether it was just echoing in her mind she could not tell.

Eventually her body turned from total rigidity into quivering jelly. So much so that if Gary's hands hadn't held her she would have collapsed on to the floor. But they did. His steel fingers supported her weight. He had let her orgasm run its course, but now he was beginning to move, stroking his cock in and out almost imperceptibly at first. Then the movement became more marked. He pulled out of her further, until his glans was almost at the opening of her vagina, then thrust all the way back in, slowly but powerfully.

'Oh god, Gary, you feel so good.' The aftermath of orgasm drained away sufficiently for her to be able to register individual feelings again. The outward stroke of his cock created a great void in her, the inner a wonderful sense of fulfilment. He filled her like no other man had. She knew what she wanted now to make her fulfilment complete. She wanted his spunk. She needed it. What made this realisation even more exhilarating was that she could feel, with every millimetre of her sex, that she was going to get precisely what she wanted and very soon.

As he slid into her, the slick of her juices making the penetration frictionless, she used all the muscles of her sex to squeeze his phallus. She felt it react immediately, jerking against his silken grip. She waited until he was right up in her again, up beyond the secret barrier, up where she had never been touched before, then squeezed for a second time. It produced another convulsion in his cock, matched, to her surprise, by an equal shock of pleasure in her.

She had never had sex like this. Even before the complex rituals indulged in by David, sex had been studied and artful, an exercise in self-knowledge and self-discipline, in getting men to do to her what she had discovered she liked most, then planning how to please them in return. She insisted on foreplay, on having her nipples stroked and her clitoris caressed. This was entirely different. He hadn't touched her nipples. She hadn't even taken off her bra. Her clitoris, though throbbing and more alive than she'd ever known it, remained neglected. It didn't appear to matter. As surely as day follows night she was going to come again the moment he ejaculated, because she knew she would be able to feel it happen as graphically as she'd ever felt anything.

He was hammering into her now, his own need asserting itself. Each inward thrust was so powerful it almost took her breath away, each threatening to make her lose control again. But she hung on by her metaphorical fingernails, clinging to the cliff face of consciousness, determined to feel him come.

Suddenly he stopped, jamming his erection into the depths of her body, pulling her back on him. He looked down at her bottom, the silky white panties stretched out all askew across her buttocks, the gusset bunched up at one side of her sex, its elastic biting into the softness of her flesh. His cock twitched, kicking against the tight, wet tube that surrounded it so sensually. It twitched again and a huge spurt of semen jetted out of him, spattering into her body, followed by another and another and another.

This time Clare was sure that she screamed. Though she had been prepared for it, though she'd felt his cock convulsing inside her, the heat and strength of his spending took her by surprise. His spunk was hot, burning inside her. She could feel every drop of it, every spot where it splattered out instantly transformed into a seething mass of raw nerves. She came as she knew she would, her second orgasm just as deep and affecting as the first, her body shuddering. She clung to the edge of the bath for support.

'Didn't even take my dress off,' she said, wanting to say something and not capable of thinking of anything else. She felt totally confused. As he pulled out of her she suffered a renewed tremor of sensation, like an orgasm in miniature. It added to her sense of bewilderment. Now that their passion was spent, its suddennness and intensity burnt out, there was a gaping emotional vacuum. She had gone so far away from anything that passed as normal behaviour for her, that it was difficult to get back into character, to re-establish the essential bearings of her life again. She sat on the edge of the bath, facing him.

'Sorry,' she said, 'I'm feeling a little shaky.'

She was looking at his body. He did remind her of the stripper. She suddenly had a vision of that tight black bottom bucking up and down on the pretty blonde. She shuddered.

'I'll take that as a compliment,' he said. He picked up a towel and began to dry his body, still wet from the shower.

'It is one,' she said.

'Another satisfied customer. I'll have to put in for more overtime from Wickesy.'

It took a moment for her to realise he was joking. 'Worth every penny,' she said weakly.

'What now?'

She needed to shower. Her body felt sticky. But she was suddenly shy. He had taken her more profoundly than any man she could remember and yet she felt inhibited about taking her dress off in front of him. She scolded herself for being silly and unbuttoned the dress quickly.

'Turn the water on,' she said, as she unclipped her white bra, trying not to feel self-conscious.

59

'You look great,' he observed.

The panties were still pulled to one side. She skimmed them down her legs and stepped into the bath as he turned the water on. The lukewarm water felt good.

'Do you want me to go?' He was watching the water flow over her firm, round breasts.

'No.'

'Do you want to go and get something to eat?'

The water refreshed her. She thought she could feel wetness – hers or his? – leaking on to her thigh. She washed it away with the soap. 'Yes, that's a good idea.' But there was a better one, as far as she was concerned, a much better one, though whether he'd be able to oblige again she did not know.

She got out of the bath and towelled herself dry, then took his hand and led him through to the bedroom.

'I can't go anywhere posh,' he said. 'Not in that clobber.'

'I could order take-away,' she suggested.

'There's something I'd like to fucking take away,' he said fiercely. He grabbed her hand and pulled her into his arms with such force it nearly knocked the breath out of her. His lips mashed against hers as he squirmed against her nakedness, his chest squashing her breasts. This was a new experience. She wrapped her arms around him and hugged him to her. His body felt wonderful, every inch as hard as steel. What was more surprising was that his cock was unfurling rapidly against her belly. By the time he broke the kiss it was as erect as it had been before.

'God, you're enthusiastic,' she said. She was having trouble believing he could recover so quickly, but there was the evidence right in front of her eyes. Not that she was complaining.

'That's your fault,' he said, glancing at his cock.

'You certainly make a woman feel desired.'

She dropped to her knees. Unsubtly, with no preliminaries, she sucked his cock into her mouth. A few minutes ago she had felt befuddled and disorientated. But she had recovered as quickly as he so evidently had. He moaned as she took him deep in her throat, cramming as much of him into her as she could.

'Great,' he mumbled.

She sucked again, feeling his cock react with a jerk. His hardness and his size made her sex throb. She began bobbing her head up and down on him, wondering if she could make him come, enamoured of the idea of feeling him come in her mouth.

'No . . .' he gasped after a moment or two. 'That's not what I want.'

He stooped and plucked her off the floor, gathering her in his arms, taking her bodily, and literally throwing her on the bed, the impression of where she had lain earlier still held in the quilt. Before she could register anything else, he had fallen on her, forced her legs apart, and stabbed his erection into her. There was no resistance. Her sex was wet. Soaking wet. No doubt part of her liquidity was his previous spending but she knew this frantic assault was arousing her strongly. Being wanted like this, being desired so ardently, must be the most powerful aphrodisiac in the world.

His right hand squeezed between their bodies to grasp her breast. He pinched her nipple. This time his tactics were entirely different. He didn't tease her. He didn't thrust into her and hold himself there. He simply hammered into her, using all his athleticism to pound his large cock into her sex, stroking it back and forth with a speed and power that she found hard to believe anyone could sustain for long. But he did. He went on and on.

Clare's orgasm, she supposed, was instantaneous, the urgency of his first thrust provoking an enormous release of feelings. But, though he must have felt her sex contracting around him and her body trembling, and heard the little mewing noises she made, he did not pause. He just hammered on, as hard and as efficiently as before, each inward stroke filling her completely, taking his cock deeper into her sex, opening her, until it felt almost as if it were splitting her. He hammered her into another orgasm that made the first pale into insignificance, then on, through that into a third, at which point she lost the last vestige of control. She wasn't really sure what happened after that, whether she just kept coming, whether she had orgasm after orgasm, or whether her body was just so prone, so helplessly vulnerable and exposed that the sensations she was experiencing, the acute pleasures, were in fact one superabundant climax.

In the middle of it all – or was it at the end, she could not tell – she felt him come too. But she was too far gone to respond. Where before she had felt every jet of his ejaculation, now it was reduced to a vague awareness of his cock bucking inside her, and a new flood of wetness seeping into her sex. She could not cope with anything else. Her body had raised its defences, saturation point reached. It was something she'd never felt before.

How long it was before he stopped, before his

pistoning buttocks came to rest, and he rolled off her, finally sated, she did not know. But almost as soon as he had, exhausted and overwhelmed physically and emotionally, Clare fell asleep. When she awoke he had gone.

# Chapter Three

'MORNING, MRS MARKHAM.' George Wickes smiled courteously.

'Morning, Mr Wickes.' Clare was on her way out of the front door.

'Everything all right? Just come to check up, as usual.'

'Everything's fine. Really taking shape now.' The carpenters had fitted the floor of the new kitchen and bathroom and were busy installing the new kitchen units.

'Should be finished tomorrow. Then you can start to get back to normal.'

Gary Newby had not turned up at the house since their night together on Tuesday. She remembered him saying he wasn't coming in the next day, but it was Friday and there was still no sign of him. She didn't have his number or address.

'That'll be wonderful. Ah, while you're here – I just wondered . . .' She didn't know how to put it.

'Yes?' He looked worried, as though there was going to be a problem with the work.

'Gary. I just wondered if Gary would be coming in again.'

'Should be. He's on another job at the moment. He'll be here to finish up tomorrow, though.'

'Oh.' Tomorrow was no good. She had accepted an invitation to David Allston's country seat for the weekend. She would have done anything to get out of it, but couldn't think of a good enough excuse. Besides, she was going to take the opportunity to tell him that, as far as she was concerned, their affair had to end. Even without the incredible sexual experience with Gary she had decided David had to go; *with* it any last doubts about the rightness of her decision had been brushed aside. She hadn't the slightest idea if she was going to have a relationship with Gary but that wasn't the point. The point was that he had shown her that she needed something entirely different when it came to sex, and it was something she very definitely was not getting from Viscount Bonmouth, and would never get.

'Nothing wrong, I hope?'

'No. It's just that I . . . I promised to lend him a book and I won't be here tomorrow, I'm going away for the weekend.'

'That's all right. Give it to me. I'll see he gets it.'

'No. I mean . . . it's all right. I'll leave it out for him.'

'Yes, that's it. Leave it on one of the new units in the kitchen.'

Damn him, she thought. She could hardly ask Wickes for Gary's telephone number.

'He'll definitely be here tomorrow?'

'Definitely. Got to get all the rubbish out and in that skip and have the skip taken away. Then the decorator can start on Monday.'

'I'd better rush.' She looked at her watch. She couldn't afford to be late today of all days. Bridget Goldsmith had flown in last night and had arranged to meet her first thing this morning.

'Don't worry about a thing. You won't recognise the place on Monday morning.'

'Thank you.'

'And don't forget that book.'

She looked puzzled for a moment, having forgotten her own lie. 'Book?'

'For Gary.'

'Oh. Right. I won't. I won't . . .' She dived through the front door and out to her car.

'She's waiting in your office,' Janice said. 'Apparently she's been in since eight thirty.'

'Jet lag.' Clare looked at the clock on the office wall. It was two minutes to nine. At lease *she* wasn't late.

'Here goes, then.'

She opened her office door. Bridget Goldsmith was sitting on the grey sofa that lined the wall opposite Clare's desk. She was reading one of the briefing files on the European launch.

'Clare, how punctual,' she said, getting to her feet. She extended her hand. Her fingers were long and bony and each one was beringed. Two gold bracelets clinked against each other as she shook Clare's hand.

'Nice to see you again, Bridget; you're looking well.'

They had only met once before, at the KissCo conference in New York. Though they had barely exchanged a word on that occasion, Bridget's personality had made a strong impression on Clare. She had worked her way up through

66

KissCo and had expanded the company's worth by fifty per cent since she took over two years ago. She was a woman who knew what she wanted and was used to getting it.

'Thank you. So do you. The air at the top obviously suits you.'

Bridget was on the thin side of slender. She had a huge mane of chestnut-coloured hair and very dark green eyes, set in a rather small, slightly pinched face. Her skin was tanned. She had never been seen wearing anything but white, with white accessories and hundredweights of gold jewellery, necklaces, bracelets, brooches and rings. Today she was wearing a white safari suit, white high-heeled shoes with a gold motif set on the toes, and a large gold medallion dangling down between her rather small breasts.

'This is good work,' she said, sitting down again and tapping the file. 'Very good work.'

'Thank you. Would you like some coffee?'

'Just hot water with a slice of lemon. Never use coffee.'

'Of course.' Clare sat behind her desk and ordered the beverages from Janice. 'So where do you want to begin?'

'Before we get down to the nitty-gritty . . .'

'Yes?' Clare said, having no idea what was coming next.

'As this is my first time in London I thought you might be able to arrange a few outings for me.'

'Of course. What sort of outings?'

'I'm just mad about history. It's the one thing America doesn't have.'

'History?'

'I don't mean buildings or museums or anything like that. What I'd really like to do is meet some genuine relics.' She laughed at her own joke. Laughter was not something that came easily to her and the sound she made was more like a horse braying. As Clare was still looking puzzled, she added, 'You know, royalty. Like Lady Di.'

'You want to meet Princess Diana?'

'Is that possible?'

'I doubt it. Not at such short notice. In fact, I think she's abroad.'

'Charles, then.'

'Ah, same problem. They're booked up months in advance.'

'Oh dear. What about a duke, then? I'd really like to meet a real live aristo. Someone with pedigree. I never have. Never even met a knight.'

Clare's secretary knocked on the door. She put the drinks down on Clare's desk and retreated without a word.

'I thought my office had made all this clear.' The tone of Bridget's voice became accusatory. If Bridget's wishes were not fulfilled it would be Clare who would be blamed.

'I suppose . . .' Clare was thinking aloud. She had planned to use this weekend to tell David Allston that there was no future in their relationship. For that reason she hesitated. It would be no problem to ask David to entertain Bridget. He was definitely a 'real live aristo' and could explain his family history in great detail to her. He might even be persuaded to introduce her to one or two of his aristocratic friends. The trouble was that if she did that, Clare would be obligated to him and could hardly tell him the bad news.

'Suppose what?' Bridget promoted.

Clare didn't have any choice. If this week went badly, if Bridget wanted to be bloody minded, she

68

could go back to Houston and give the European launch to the Paris office and Claude Duhamel. In a matter of months the English operation could be run from France and Clare would end up being the managing director of a warehouse and distribution operation.

'Would a viscount do?'

'Duke, earl, viscount, baron, lord. That's it, isn't it? Gee, a viscount would be just fine.'

She'd missed out marquesses, but Clare didn't correct her. 'Viscount Bonmouth. Created 1781.'

'Five years after the start of the War of Independence,' Bridget said in an awed tone.

'Yes. He's a friend of mine. He's got a house in London and a country estate in Hertfordshire. I'm sure I could wangle an invitation to dinner.'

'Gee, I'd be real honoured.'

Clare appeared to have scored a gold star, several gold stars. 'I'm seeing him tonight. I'll ask.' She was trapped. There was no going back now. She'd just have to delay the inevitable. She felt bad about that, but not that bad.

It had been another long day. Bridget had not left her for a second, reviewing every aspect of KissCo's UK operation as well as the details of the European launch, though the formal presentation was not until Monday. Her reputation for thoroughness was well-founded. She'd gone through every detail. They hadn't stopped for lunch but had sandwiches sent in, and it was well after seven before Bridget announced she was going back to her hotel.

As Clare drove her BMW along the A40 she experienced a wave of exhaustion. She turned the air-conditioning on to full blast to refresh her, and

looked at the dashboard clock. It was eight
fifteen. It would be at least an hour before she
reached Althorp House. She punched David's
number into the car phone.

'Is David there?' she asked.

'Hold on, ma'am.' The butler had answered the
phone and recognised her voice.

'Clare?'

'David. I'm running late.'

'No problem,' he said. 'How long?'

'An hour.'

'So shall I get them to hold dinner?'

'Just a snack would be fine.' The thought of
eating an elaborate meal served in the baronial
dining room by David's obsequious servants was
not appealing. The idea of the whole weekend was
becoming truly unattractive. She knew David
would have spent the week planning one of his
elaborate sexual charades, and then there would
be dinner for the county set on Saturday night. But
now she could do nothing but grin and bear it.

An hour and a half later she was sitting in front
of a grand Gothic fireplace in the dining room of
the House. The dining table could seat sixty, but
only one end was set with places for two and a
selection of cold cuts, smoked salmon, salads and
bread which Clare consumed eagerly, discovering
that she was hungrier than she'd thought.

David sat opposite her, picking more desul-
torily at the food. His body language, coiled and
nervous, suggested a child on Christmas Eve, his
eyes sparkling with anticipation while he tried to
remain ostensibly calm. Clare didn't need to
guess why he was in such a state.

'Look, perhaps you're too tired,' he said, aware
of her languor. He said it in the tone of a man who

was prepared to cut his own throat but hoped it would not be necessary.

'No, I'm fine,' Clare replied lamely. 'I'm feeling better now I've had something to eat.'

'Oh good.' David looked relieved. He had spent a great deal of time creating tonight's scenario and most of the week anticipating it. But he was a gentleman first and foremost, and if Clare had said she was too tired he would have had to delay his gratification with as much good grace as he could muster. 'Take your time, take your time,' he said. 'More wine?'

She nodded. He poured the white wine into her crystal glass.

'So who is this Bridget?' he asked.

Clare had broached the subject at the beginning of the meal. 'My boss. Boss of bosses. *Le grand fromage.*' She sipped the wine. Oddly, she found herself thinking about Gary, perhaps because she was becoming increasingly aware of what awaited her upstairs. The contrast between the spontaneous, cataclysmic sex she had enjoyed with him and David's calculated, scripted games was marked. She wondered where he was now. Was he giving some other woman the benefit of his considerable prowess? She shuddered at the thought.

'You're not cold, are you?'

'No. Just someone running over my grave,' she countered, trying to chase Gary's phantom away.

'It's been so warm.'

'I'm not cold really. This is delicious.' She stabbed another piece of smoked salmon and dragged it on to her plate.

'So this woman wants to meet an aristocrat?'

'Yes. Would you mind?'

'Of course not. Does she want to come here or

71

the London house?'

'Doesn't matter.'

'I'll organise something. Actually, next Friday I was going to have a little gathering in London. I was going to ask you to come. I suppose she could come too. The Duke of Tidmouth's going to be there. That might impress her.'

'Perfect. That's very kind of you.' She touched his arm.

'There's puddings,' he said with reluctance, obviously hoping she wouldn't want any, anxious to get on with the main business of the evening.

'No. Nothing else. Well, a coffee perhaps.'

'Absolutely.'

The butler was summoned and a maid cleared away. Coffee arrived in a Georgian silver pot on a Georgian silver tray with white, bone-china cups. The butler poured Clare a cup, knowing her preference for black coffee with no sugar.

'Thank you,' she said.

'Ma'am,' he replied curtly, leaving them alone once more.

Clare sipped the coffee and looked across at David. Now that they were only minutes away from realising his plans his excitement was visible.

Her feelings were more ambiguous. Gary's impact on her life had been more affecting than she would have imagined. She had tried to shunt aside her thoughts about him and what he had done to her, to catalogue it as casual sex that, while satisfying, did not touch the main stream of her life. But it was not as easy as that. Over the last three days she had found herself daydreaming about him in graphic detail, every moment, every second of their encounter vividly replayed.

She could see it, feel it, even taste what it had been like. She could remember exactly how he had felt as he plunged into her vagina, precisely how he had held her effortlessly in his arms. It was like she had been given a wonderful present, which she could take out and examine with huge delight whenever she felt the urge.

The urge had become urgent. Twice since Tuesday night Clare had masturbated and on both occasions had come ferociously as she relived the experience with the builder. She had deliberately recreated the conditions, masturbating in the bathroom, bent over the side of the bath. She masturbated on the bed. Both the places he had taken her. Usually she could extend her masturbation rites for a long time, luxuriating in the feelings she created, but the thoughts of Gary had provoked her too powerfully, and her orgasms had been achieved in no time at all.

She sipped her coffee, wondering what David had dreamed up for tonight. If Bridget had not intervened she might well have decided to use this moment to tell him their relationship was over, get in her car and drive back to London, ready for Gary's arrival first thing in the morning. But now that was impossible. If she could tip the scales against Paris by introducing Bridget to a real viscount then she had no qualms about doing it. She hoped the French Revolution had effectively reduced the chances of Claude being able to compete in this area.

It meant she felt obliged to go through with David's plans for tonight. Actually she supposed she could have used the time-honoured excuse of a headache. But there were two reasons she couldn't do that. One was the way he was looking at her, like a puppy-dog waiting to be told it could jump onto its master's lap. The other was her own need. She needed sex. She needed it badly. She would much rather have had Gary. She would much rather have him carry her upstairs and throw her on to the bed and proceed to ravish her as totally as he had on Tuesday night. But Gary wasn't on offer. David was. And needs must when the devil drives . . .

'Do you want more coffee?' David asked.

'No.' She looked into his eyes, brushing the tip of her forefinger across her bottom lip.

'Or a brandy?' He didn't want to be the one to suggest it was time for bed.

'No, David. I think it's time we went upstairs now, don't you?'

'I'd like that,' he said. 'I just . . .' He hesitated.

'Just what?'

'If it's . . . I mean . . .' A cloud had passed over his face. 'If it's too much . . .'

Clare looked at him intently. 'If *what's* too much?'

'I don't want you to do anything you're not comfortable with.'

'I won't,' she said, getting to her feet. 'Give me twenty minutes.' She needed more time tonight. She wanted to shower first.

'Right,' he agreed, looking at his watch.

She walked up to the bedroom she had been allotted, a vast room on the first floor, over-looking the carriage driveway at the front of the house. It was appropriately called the blue room, although the name came from the colour scheme of the walls, carpet and upholstery rather than any sexual connotation.

Clare shut the door behind her. One of the

maids had unpacked the few items she had hurriedly grabbed from her house after work, and hung them in a vast walnut wardrobe. There was an equally imposing four-poster bed, the posts elaborately carved, its drapes a heavy and rather dull brocade. As she had expected, there were the usual gift-wrapped parcels on the bed, but this time there were three of them which David had sneaked away during dinner to deliver.

Judging from what David had said downstairs, the script for tonight's interlude was a little more complicated than anything he had suggested before. Clare was intrigued despite herself.

Clare stripped off her clothes. She walked into the cavernous and old-fashioned bathroom, the cast-iron and self-standing bath, the toilet with an overhead cistern and a chain. Incongruously, a modern shower cubicle had been installed in one corner. Showering quickly, Clare towelled herself dry on a large, fluffy white bath towel and went back into the bedroom.

She took the small square box and placed it on the bedside table, then tore the gold wrappings from the larger rectangular box. Inside were the usual layers of white tissue paper. Searching among them Clare pulled out a white lace unitard – a nylon leotard and tights combined into one garment. A neatly hemmed hole had been cut out where the crotch should be. The box also contained a pair of white, patent-leather high-heels.

The letter was at the bottom of the box. She unfolded the single sheet of paper and read the italic script. All was revealed. David's fantasies had always followed a pattern. They featured two themes, which Clare recognised from her own extensive reading on the subject of sexual behaviour. The first was what the books liked to call submission. He wanted her to dominate him. The second was an element of transvestism. David liked to wear women's clothes, more precisely, their underwear. Whether this was a separate strand of his sexuality or part of his desire to be submissive, Clare did not know or care. But it was there. She had often wondered if he dressed as a woman on his own, not just in silky knickers but in full drag, with tights, shoes, sock-filled bras, a dress and a wig. It was perfectly possible, she thought.

Each letter, each of the rituals they'd played out, developed these two themes, extending them, getting closer, Clare suspected, to the re-enactment of the event that had begun this strange sexual obsession. Tonight he had suggested another step towards it, though she was sure, from what he'd said, he considered it a giant leap. It explained why the third gold-wrapped box was long and thin.

Clare picked up the white lace and climbed into it. She pulled it up, smoothing it out over her legs. The upper half had full sleeves and a deep V-neckline, the tight material flattening her breasts slightly. The fact that the garment left her entire sex exposed, from the top of her labia at the front to the little crater of her anus at the back, made her feel quite aroused. The arousal was welcome. She wasn't sure she would have been able to cope with what David wanted her to do without it.

She slotted her feet into the shoes. The four-inch spiky heels tipped her feet into a sharp angle. She took her make-up out of her bag and quickly darkened her eye-shadow and refreshed her mascara and lipstick. She was not sure how she felt about doing what David had suggested. A good part of her, a part she would have to hold at bay, was not at all sure she wanted to go through with it. The rest of her could be persuaded, if reluctantly, that it might be exciting.

The tentative tap on the door came at exactly the appointed time. She wondered if he'd been standing outside counting the seconds.

'Come.'

He'd expected her to be sitting on the edge of the bed but she stood by the cheval-glass in one corner of the room. He could see the semi-transparent lace stretched over her slender, curvaceous body from the front, and in the mirror he could see the back too, the contours of her tight, round buttocks firmed by the high heels.

'Well,' she said. 'You know what to do.'

David hastily got to his knees. He was wearing a short, white, cotton robe.

'Good.' she went over to the edge of the bed and sat down. 'Now come here.'

He shuffled towards her on his knees as he had done so many times before. She saw his cock begin to protrude from the front of the white cotton.

'Faster,' she urged impatiently.

He arrived within a foot of her.

'Take your robe off.'

Immediately he tore the robe off his shoulders. His body seemed effeminate but then, she knew, she was comparing it to the rugged muscles of Gary's powerful physique. David's phallus was not as large either, though it was now fully erect.

She raised her legs and pressed the little horseshoe-shaped steel heel of the shoe into his right nipple. He gasped.

Clare's mood was changing rapidly. She began to feel a certain anger at the way she was being used. She tried to fight it back, using the sexual need she felt so strongly to keep it at bay.

'What do you want, David?' she asked.

'You know what I want,' he said in a whisper. this wasn't in the script.

'Yes, I think I do. You see that.' She pointed at her clothes. She had folded them neatly over a small boudoir chair. 'I want you to get my knickers.'

He looked puzzled and even a little alarmed. She had never varied the game to this extent. The underwear he was supposed to put on was in the drawer of the bedside table. But he decided against saying anything and crawled over to the chair. Clare had been wearing small bikini pants in black satin. He picked them up. They still carried a vestige of her body heat.

'You know what to do.'

'You want me to put them on?' The surprise in his voice was streaked with excitement.

'Yes.'

He got to his feet. His hands were trembling. He pulled the black satin up over his legs and hips. The panties were too narrow to completely cover his erection, so the upper half stuck out over the top. As he smoothed the material out he made a low breathy sound, the result of extreme excitement. He'd never imagined she would allow him to do this.

'Do they feel nice?'

'Oh yes,' he said passionately. 'So soft, so silky.'

'Come back here.'

When he was kneeling in front of her again she

tossed the long rectangular box on the floor. 'Open it,' she ordered.

He ripped off the gold foil and opened the box. It contained a long, thin riding crop with a braided leather handle. At the tip of the whip was a thick loop of leather.

'Give it to me!' she demanded, holding out her hand. He handed her the whip.

'Right, now get the blindfold.'

He did as he was told, taking the box from the bedside table, unwrapping it and extracting the black, silk sleeping-mask. She pointed to the spot in front of her and he crawled back to it. The elasticated waist of her panties was cutting across his erection, digging into the flesh.

Clare held the whip in her hand. She had read about men – and women for that matter – who had a penchant for receiving corporal punishment and others who were equally turned on by administrating it. She had never had any desire to experience either. But the anger she had felt earlier seemed to be able to flow out of her through the whip. If this is what David wanted she could use her anger to satisfy his needs.

'Put the blindfold on, David,' she ordered. She wasn't following the script at all, but judging from the state of his erection he didn't mind in the least. He slipped the silk over his eyes.

Clare lifted her foot to his nipple, using the pointed toe to prod it this time. Tentatively, as if he expected a rebuke at any moment, he raised his hand to her foot, gently bringing it up to his lips, then kissing and licking at the white leather. Resting her foot on his shoulder, as she had done before, she held up her other foot for the same treatment.

'You'd better do a good job,' she said. There was a line like that in his script. He wanted to be punished for failing to please her. Was that what the maid, who Clare suspected had been at the bottom of his obsessions, had done to him all those years ago? Had it been her sadism that had started all this? Or was the maid just a figment of Clare's imagination?

David's mouth was working up along her thigh. She crossed her ankles around the back of his neck, spreading her legs apart, her labia opening. 'Do it,' she said, not wanting to wait while he inched his way up her leg. He'd given her the power to command, so why shouldn't she use it?

Instantly his mouth plunged on to her sex, his tonguing darting up to her clitoris. She felt a surge of pleasure. God, he was good at this. Unbelievably good. He seemed to have an unerring ability to find the spot that produced the most intense sexual feelings, and manipulate it with just the right pressure and the perfect rhythm. It was wonderful. Wonderful. It was what she needed badly. She allowed herself to wallow in it, an orgasm swelling in her like the overture of an opera, sensual and gentle, not sharp and intense.

'Stop that,' she commanded, the moment it was over.

He stopped immediately.

'Not very good, is it?' she lied. That corresponded to his script.

'No. I'm sorry.'

'You're going to be.' The script again. 'Get on all fours.' She got to her feet. She imagined the young maid exercising her power over the young master, realising he was becoming increasingly involved in her games. Without thinking about it too much she raised the crop and slashed it down across the black satin that was stretched tightly across his buttocks.

'Oh my god,' he moaned. His whole body quivered.

'Again?'

'Yes, yes . . .'.

She stroked the whip down again. It hit harder this time. He groaned loudly. Without asking she applied a third cut. This time his groan was squeezed out between clenched teeth. She saw his whole body go rigid and shake convulsively. There was little doubt that he had come.

How long was it, she wondered, since he'd dared to ask a woman to do this to him? Had he ever dared ask? Clare realised that she didn't care.

Quietly she walked around to the side of the bed and lay down. The ambiguity she had felt earlier had not gone away. Had it not been for a raging sexual need, she would have walked out on him whatever the consequences. But she was determined to have her own needs satisfied. She felt dirty. She hoped an explosive orgasm would wash her clean.

'Give me the blindfold,' she said, her voice level and unemotional. She held out her hand without looking up at him and felt the silk folding into her fingers. Quickly she fitted the sleeping-mask over her own eyes. The blackness was a wonderful relief, offering her anonymity. She spread her legs apart, wishing she had taken the time to strip off the ridiculous bodystocking.

David didn't have to be told what to do. She felt his weight shifting on the bed. He knelt between her legs, kissing her inner thigh until he reached her labia. His mouth sucked at her sex, making her moan. He dipped his tongue into her vagina, pressing it surprisingly deeply and wriggling it around. Then he moved up to her clitoris, finding the magic spot, stroking it with that perfectly measured rhythm, tonguing the little nub of flesh from side to side.

The waves of sensation David had always created in her began to change her mood, excitement reasserting itself over her disgust.

'Oh god,' she moaned, snapping her head to one side. And then, unbidden, he walked across the screen in her mind. 'Yes,' she said aloud. It was Gary. Naked. Tall. Erect. A smile flicked around his mouth, as he looked at her, a knowing smile, knowing her need.

Her body reacted with a huge surge of feeling as David's artful tongue worked on her clitoris. She knew she was going to come. She could feel Gary's body in her arms as hard as steel, pressing down on her, squeezing her breasts as that big cock nudged at the entrance to her sex. 'Yes, yes,' she encouraged.

She tossed her head from side to side wildly, lifting her buttocks off the bed, angling her sex up to him, wanting him more than any man. The phantom timed it perfectly. As the frequency of the waves of feeling got shorter, the time between the crests of pleasure reducing rapidly, and the explosion of orgasm crashed through her body, Gary surged into her, filling her, stretching her, making her whole again. Her body locked, her thighs clamped around David's head.

'Darling, darling, darling,' she cried, her body trembling helplessly.

# Chapter Four

'*GARY?*'

'Who is this?'

'Clare.'

'Clare?'

'Clare Markham. You're standing in my house, remember?'

In the middle of a very disturbed night's sleep Clare had suddenly realised how she could contact Gary. He would be working in her house on Saturday morning and might answer the phone. She'd dialled her own number at nine o'clock in the morning.

'Oh right, Ms Markham.' He sounded distant and unfriendly.

'Clare,' she corrected. 'I didn't have your number,' she explained.

'My number.' He sounded puzzled now.

'Yes, so I could ring you.'

'Why would you want to ring me?'

That was not the reaction she'd been expecting. 'After Tuesday night I thought that might be obvious.'

'Oh.'

83

'Gary, you *do* remember?' she asked with alarm.

'Yeah sure,' he said noncommittally.

'Well?'

'Well what?'

'I'd like to see you again.'

His tone changed. 'Really?' he said brightly.

'Of course,' she replied. 'Did you think I wouldn't?'

'Yeah.'

'After what happened between us?'

'I just thought . . .'

'What?'

'You know . . . it was just, like, a one off.'

'God, Gary, it was wonderful. Wonderful. Didn't you think so?'

'Yeah. It was great. But you're a posh lady. I thought when you woke up in the morning. Well you know. I'm only a bricky. That's why I left.'

'We established every woman you've ever worked with has thrown themselves at you, right?'

He laughed that lovely laugh. 'Yeah, right.'

'Well I'm throwing myself again. Will you have dinner with me tonight?'

'Is that what you want?'

'Very much.'

'Where are you now?'

'I had to go to a girlfriend's last night.'

'Right. By the way, it's nearly finished. Another couple of hours. They're putting the carpets back right now. It looks great. What time will you be home?'

'Afternoon.'

'I've got to get home and change.'

'Good, so come around seven.'

'Great.'

'See you.'

'See you.'

He was right, Clare thought – it was great.

'Can't be helped. I'm really sorry.'

'That's all right. When did she call?'

'She called me on my mobile. There's nothing I can do about it, David.'

They were sitting on the terrace overlooking the sweeping lawns of gardens rumoured to have been created by Capability Brown. A large table had been set with a white linen cloth and a lavish breakfast.

'That's perfectly all right. You'll stay to lunch.' He was being remarkably understanding about it.

'Of course, I'd love to. As long as I'm back in town by three. She wants to go over our whole campaign strategy.'

'Well, ask her if she'll come to dinner with us all next Friday, will you?'

'That's very kind of you, David.' His kindness was making her feel guilty about lying. Not guilty enough to want to change her mind, however.

'And mention Philip.'

'Philip?'

'The Duke of Tidmouth. That should get you extra brownie points.'

'He really is a duke?'

'Yes. Created 1654. That'll impress her.'

'I'm sure it will.'

Clare was treading a delicate line. On the one hand she wanted to tell David the truth and drive back to London as fast as she could. From the way she had treated him last night, Clare was surprised David hadn't already guessed the truth. The truth was that she had crossed an invisible line when it came to her idea of what was and what was not acceptable. The disgust she had felt was not pleasant and not something she wanted to repeat. She was determined never to play any of David's games again. Never.

On the other hand, since David appeared not to realise how she felt, it suited her interests not to charge in with both feet and spell out her indignation. To be fair to him, he had tried to warn her that what he had planned might be one step too far. If she had not been so wrapped up in her own need for sexual gratification, she could have simply said no. She liked David. He was a gentleman. But his sexual obsessions were becoming more pronounced. If there had been a maid, or some other woman in the household, who had entertained him illicitly for her own pleasure, she had certainly left an indelible mark on him.

'So what do you want to do before lunch?' he asked. 'The pool's a lovely temperature. Or we could go for a ride?'

They had done a really good job. Not only had George Wickes kept his promise of being finished on time, but his men had cleared up the dust sheets, replaced the furniture and carpets, and cleaned the house. In fact, the house was so clean, from top to bottom, Clare wondered if he'd employed a specialist firm to scrub it out.

There was still the decoration to be done, of course. The new kitchen and bathroom had to be tiled, and her bedroom and the dining room where the walls had been knocked through had to be repainted. But that would be completed in a few days and would cause little mess. In short, her house belonged to her again.

It was four by the time she got home. Lots of time to get ready for Gary. She decided to start by taking a bath. As the new walls around the new bath were untiled she thought it would be wiser to use the old bathroom.

In the bath she lay quietly trying to sort out her thoughts and emotions. Such a lot had happened in a short space of time. There was Bridget and the presentation. They had not, as yet, discussed Clare's ideas on the advertising campaign for the launch, which she knew were diametrically opposed to the American's. That was a battle yet to be fought. Although taking her to meet David and a 'real live' duke would be a considerable coup, Clare was not naive enough to believe that Bridget's reputation for being a hard-nosed business woman would allow such incidentals actually to sway her final decision.

Whatever else happened on Friday night, however, Clare was determined she wasn't going to get into another situation where she was expected to perform with and for David. Somehow she would have to finesse her way out of that. And, at a later date, tell him what she had intended to tell him this weekend, that enough was very definitely enough.

She wondered if Gary had affected her feelings. Had sex with Gary not been so extraordinary would she have felt such disgust at David's demands? She had seen David through Gary's eyes, his sexual foibles forming part of the decadence of the aristocracy as against the dignity and simplicity of the working class. Clare smiled. She was even introducing British class distinctions into her sex life.

The thought of Gary made her heart leap. It

was ridiculous. She was behaving like a love-sick schoolgirl, like she had in the fifth form at school over Andrew Jenkins. She'd developed such a crush on the one-year-older sixth former that every time she saw him across the playground it would send her into hopeless paroxysms of joy, fear, embarrassment and sexual excitement, a cocktail of emotions that left her drained and weak.

But, unlike with Gary, she had never managed to have her wicked way with Andrew Jenkins, despite a few attempts to lure him into the copse at the side of the school playing-fields. Her passion for Gary was based on altogether more solid ground. The thought of what he had done to her created a deep pulse in her sex, right up in the centre of it, a pulse she felt she could put her finger on if she pressed hard enough just under her belly button. It reminded her of that odd feeling she had experienced as he powered into her, the way he had seemed to break through to a part of her sex that had never been encroached on before. That was where the pulse emanated from, that was where he had left his mark on her.

She sat up, the water washing off her breasts. Almost unconsciously she had been grinding her thighs together and her clitoris, trapped between her labia, was beginning to respond. She looked down at her nipples and saw they had knitted themselves into little, hard, puckered buds of corrugated flesh.

'Damn,' she said aloud. She stood up and soaped her body vigorously, trying to ignore its demands. But the slick of lather she created only made matters worse. Everything she touched seemed to have suddenly become invested with the ability to deliver a shock of sensual pleasure. She slid down into the water, to wash all the soap away, then stood up and got out of the bath.

It attracted her like a magnet. She took a towel and dried herself off as she walked back into her old bedroom at the back of the house. She went straight to the bedside table and opened the drawer. As much as she told herself this was absurd when she expected Gary in three hours, the impulse was too strong to resist. She took out her thick, cream, plastic vibrator. It was a straight cylindrical tube, ribbed for two-thirds of its length and had a smooth, torpedo-shaped top.

In a spirit of annoyance with herself for conjuring up the spectre of Gary, Clare threw the towel aside and lay on the bed. Callously she jammed the tip of the dildo against her clitoris and turned the gnarled ring at its base to set the vibrations to maximum, in no mood for subtlety. She gasped as her clitoris erupted with sensation, the hard pulsing frequency burrowing into it.

Clare held the dildo firmly, crushing the little nut of nerves back against her pubic bone. The sensations increased. She used her other hand to gather up her left breast. Squeezing the pliant flesh she pinched her nipple between her fingers. Again, not content with temperance, she used her fingernails to create more bite. She moaned as the stab of pain shot through her body, translated instantly by her arousal to acute pleasure.

Unceremoniously, her orgasm already begin-ning to build up in her body, she caught hold of her other breast and repeated the process. Again the pain provoked by the cutting edge of her nails was turned in to hot, throbbing pleasure, taking her closer to her climax. Thinking of Gary, as she had last night, she moved the head of the dildo to the maw of her vagina. She held it there for a second, just as Gary had held his erection there the first time he'd taken her; then, not able to resist her need any longer, she plunged the dildo up into her sex. There was no resistance. It slid all the way up on a flood of juices.

The dildo was a poor substitute for the real thing but she writhed down on it, as she used her other hand to manipulate her clit.

'Gary, oh god, Gary,' she screamed aloud. She arched her buttocks off the bed, offered herself to him, to the phantom who she seemed to be unable to drive from her mind.

But even as the orgasm was unleashed, even as the shocks of feeling coursed through her body creating delicious, intoxicating pleasure, even as she jammed the dildo right up her vagina, her fingers pushing it so deep the stub-end disappeared inside her, she was aware that it had not touched that secret place, the new special place Gary had discovered in the upper reaches of her sex.

She saw his red Toyota pick-up park a little way down the street. She had been waiting, guiltily, in the front bedroom watching for it, the love-sick schoolgirl unable to do anything else.

She managed to resist the temptation to run downstairs and fling open the front door before he'd walked up the garden path. Instead she waited at the top of the stairs and walked down sedately once he'd rung the bell.

'Hi,' she said.

'Hi.'

He was wearing a crisp, white shirt and very pale, spotlessly clean jeans with a pair of dark-blue dockside shoes. He was smiling.

Clare felt her pulse race. After a few days the details of his face had faded, but if anything, he was more handsome than she remembered. In fact he was gorgeous. His blond hair was freshly washed and his chin newly shaved. He smelt of a subtle, musky aftershave. His eyes were looking at her steadily, their expression a mixture of amusement and unease.

'Come in,' she said. Clare felt a momentary embarrassment, not sure whether she should kiss him or not. He was much taller than she remembered and she would have to stretch up on tip-toe to reach, so instead she touched his arm and led him through into the sitting room. 'Would you like a drink? Glass of wine?' She realised that, despite asking him for dinner, she'd prepared no food. Food was the last thing on her mind. They'd have to eat out, hopefully much later.

'I'd prefer beer,' he said. He seemed to be a little tentative too, shifting his weight from one foot to the other.

'Sit down then. I'll go and get it.'

'What do you think of the job?' he shouted through to her as she took the beer from her new fridge. She poured a glass of red wine for herself.

'It's great. I can't believe it's all so clean.'

'That was me,' he said. He had sat in the corner of one of the two matching sofas. She handed him the bottle of beer.

'What do you mean?'

'I stayed late. It really was a mess. Didn't want you coming home to that.'

'That was very nice of you.' She sat down next to him and touched his arm. 'I thought Mr Wickes had hired a professional cleaner.' She nodded at the bottle. 'Would you rather have a glass?'

'This is fine.'

Clare realised she couldn't think of a single thing to say to him outside the subject of the work on her house. They didn't know each other well enough for silence to be comfortable, so she scratched around desperately for something to say.

'What's your next job?' she asked, finally coming up with a topic.

'Fulham. House conversion into two flats.'

'That's interesting.' It wasn't. She didn't know anything about building. 'Is it going to be difficult?' Not as difficult as this conversation she guessed.

'Not really. Except there's an architect. They're always farting around, getting in the way.'

'Really?'

'Yeah. They charge the client a fortune for what a good builder would do anyway. It's a total waste of money. I mean, look at your job here. As long as you know what you want, who needs it?'

'Right,' she said.

The silence fell again, heavy and increasingly oppressive. Clare cast around for some subject to get them out of the mire. The truth seemed to present the best approach. 'Gary,' she said. His name sounded strange. She had said it so many times in her head over the last few days but out loud it assumed a different character. 'It's not easy, is it?'

'No,' he agreed. 'I very nearly didn't come.'

'I'm glad you did. Really glad. It's just that what

happened between us . . . well, I guess our bodies sort of went on to automatic. Our minds need time to catch up.'

'Is that what it is?'

'I'm sorry.'

'What are you sorry for?'

'You don't look very comfortable about all this.'

'I'm not. You're not the sort of woman I normally . . .' He stopped. She had the feeling he was going to say 'fuck'. 'Go out with.'

'Does that matter?'

'I don't know. It feels like it matters. We ain't got much in common. I mean I can't even talk like you. You sound so posh.'

'That doesn't matter either. It doesn't mean we can't be friends, does it?'

'Is that what you want?'

'I want to get to know you, Gary. If you feel the same about me that's the basis for something, isn't it?'

'You're very good at words. I'm not. They trip me up. I don't know what you want. I thought Tuesday was, well, you know, just a one-night stand.'

'Is that what you'd like it to be? I don't want you to feel obligated.'

'No. See. That's not what I meant.'

'What then?'

It was though he was having a debate with himself, trying to work out what to say and what to do, his brow furrowed and his eyes unfocussed.

'I'm not good at this,' he said, almost to himself.

'I don't see . . .'

Before she could finish the sentence Gary caught her by the arm, twisted her round to face him and kissed her full on the mouth, his other hand clamping around her cheeks. He pressed his lips down on hers and plunged his tongue into the warm wetness beyond them. She was taken by surprise, but recovered quickly, sucking on his tongue as she wrapped her arms around his back, feeling the same electric sensations she had experienced on Tuesday night, the awkwardness between them evaporating in the heat of passion.

'Oh Gary, Gary,' she muttered without taking her mouth away from his, her lips moving against his, the words almost gagged on his tongue.

She was wearing a light-red shift. In anticipation of what she hoped would happen between them she had not worn tights, panties or a bra. As Gary's left hand slid around to the back of her neck, pressing her forward on to his mouth, his right hand travelled up between her thighs. A grunt of pure pleasure followed his discovery of her wantonness, his fingers sinking into her thinly haired labia.

Without breaking the kiss Clare twisted around slightly so she could part her legs. Immediately she felt his forefinger moving up to the fourchette of her labia, delving under the little hood of flesh to find her clitoris. The search was short. Her clitoris was hard and swollen, pulsating as though to draw attention to itself. She moaned involuntarily as his finger nudged against it.

'Please, please . . .' she tried to say, not at all sure what she was begging for. He smothered the words with his mouth, sucking on her lips hungrily.

His finger felt rough and calloused. He pressed her clitoris as though it were the button to some strange machine. She found that it was, a machine that generated such a kick of sensation that it ignited the first stirrings of orgasm. He was not at all gentle. He was not at all subtle. He merely pressed her clitoris back with the tip of his finger, then rotated it as if tracing a tiny circle. At the same time she felt the fingers of his other hand parting her labia lower down. She was wet. Embarrassingly wet. If he had any doubts about how much she wanted him they would surely be wiped away. Two fingers moved together to probe the opening of her vagina. They worked themselves against it, but did not penetrate, scissoring apart to stretch it and create a new sensation of pleasure. Her vagina felt as though it were alive, reacting to this provocation with a massive contraction.

'You're so hot,' he said as he moved his mouth down to her neck. The feeling of his lips and hot tongue lapping at her flesh made her throw her head back, the sinews of her throat corded like rope. That made it easier for him to fasten his mouth on them, sucking the skin in.

He took his hand away from her vagina momentarily and fumbled at the top of her dress, trying to pull it off her shoulders. After a minute he lost patience, grabbing the material and jerking it so roughly the strap tore away. He cleared the dress from her breasts and dropped his head on to them, taking each in turn, sucking as much of the flesh into his mouth as he could manage, then concentrating on the nipple, sawing it from side to side, against the edge of his teeth.

Clare was coming. Her whole body was quivering. Exactly as before, his assault this time had been so sudden and unexpected, even though she had hoped it would happen, that it took her completely by surprise. She wanted that wonderful cock inside her again, but just the idea of it, in conjunction with the physical ravishment he was subjecting her to, was sending her over the edge. As his teeth created a delicious torture on her nipples – pain and pleasure so co-mingled she could not separate the two – her sex seemed to catch fire, the pleasure consuming her. His hands had gone back to her sex and she forced herself down on them as best she could, wriggling her vagina against one hand and her clitoris against the other.

'So good, so good,' she told him, when she was able to form words again.

'I know.'

He had no intention of leaving it at that. Even before she had recovered, with the tentacles of orgasm still wrapped around her body, Gary slipped down on to the floor at her feet. His rough hands seized the calves and pulled her legs apart, hooking her feet over his shoulders. She was pulled forward, her buttocks hanging over the seat of the sofa. He dipped his head and pressed his mouth on her sex.

It was what David had done to her so many times and yet it could not have felt more different. She gasped. His mouth was hot, and his tongue licked her like a flame, the lightest touch a shock. He swept it all the way up between her labia in long, wide strokes, using the full breadth of his tongue. She was so sensitive, all her emotions so fevered, she thought she could feel the nodules of his tastebuds acting like sandpaper against her tender flesh. It was not unpleasant. At the moment she doubted anything he did to her could be that. It was just another new sensation to add to the catalogue of them, each sending thrills of pleasure to every nerve.

She would have liked to have time to analyse it all, as she was in the habit of doing with everything in her life. But there was no time for that and no room for it either. There was no time or space for anything but the pounding arousal that was mounting in her again. She didn't have the ability to step back from it all, and try to work out why and what he was doing to her had the effect it did.

His tongue changed position, centring on her clitoris. He pressed it back just as his finger had done. But his tongue was hot and sticky and there seemed to be a pulse in it, blood coursing through it rhythmically, the tempo of it somehow matched to the frequency of the pleasure that was throbbing in Clare's body. He didn't move it at all, as though he knew what she could feel. And that was enough. A second orgasm broke free. She gasped, her fingers gripping his blond hair, holding his head firm, the feeling he was giving her so perfect, so precise, so wonderful she couldn't have borne it if he had moved even a fraction of an inch.

It was a long time before she came down from her high. At least it felt like a long time. Time was relative in this situation, prone to the gravitational pull of unremitting passion.

'Oh Gary, what are you doing to me?' Her fingers were still twisted in his hair. She let it go, then wiped his wet mouth with one hand.

He smiled and got to his feet. He kicked off his shoes, peeled off his white socks, unbuttoned his shirt and stripped it off.

'Let me,' Clare said eagerly, the large bulge that distended the fly of his jeans right in front of her. She leant forward, unbuckled his brown leather belt and unzipped the pale denim, his erection making it difficult. She pulled his white boxer shorts and jeans down to his knees.

The sight of his cock sent a new thrill of pleasure through her. It seemed to revive all the waves of pleasure she'd already experienced, like a tuning-fork setting off all the resonances in the same key. For a moment she felt completely thrown by the tremor of feeling this created.

Then she slipped to her knees and took his erection into her mouth greedily, in no mood for delicacy, sucking and chewing on it, then forcing it deep into the back of her throat, so deep she had to control the reflex to gag. She would love to make him come like this, she realised. For all her desire to feel him ejaculate in the depths of her sex, she would love to be able to provoke him so much that he simply could not stop himself from coming in her mouth. The idea made her sex clench of its own accord.

Gary laced his fingers into her hair, just as she had done with his moments before. She strained to look up into his face without taking her mouth away, trying to tell him with her eyes what she wanted him to do. She pulled her lips back and ran her tongue around the very pronounced ridge at the base of his glans. That made his cock twitch. She did it again, then plunged her mouth down on him again, sucking so hard her cheeks were dimpled.

'You're good at that,' he said coolly.

'Love it,' she managed to say, the words gagged on his cock. She sucked on him hard again, then began to bob her head back and forth, turning her slick, wet mouth into a perfect imitation of her slick, wet sex.

Gary gasped, swaying back slightly. But she knew he was still in control. 'No,' he said quietly, but did not attempt to move away.

'Yes,' she said, pronouncing the word against his cock. She brought it almost all the way out, then slid it back in, her tongue licking the underside of the broad shaft, her hands clutching at his bare buttocks now, feeling their hard muscles. His cock pulsed, swelling in her mouth. She felt his body change subtly, his level of resistance lowering. She might still get her own way.

Clare established a rhythm, sawing her mouth to and fro with absolute regularity, making sure her lips brushed the ridge of his glans on the outward stroke and then sucked hard on the inner. Her fingers dug into his buttocks. Without breaking the tempo she moved one finger down to the cleft of his bottom and searched for the hole of his anus.

His cock was slicked with her saliva. She used her whole mouth, moulding it to him, sucking on him, wanting to make it an irresistible receptacle for his spunk. the idea of feeling him jetting over her tongue and down her throat was turning her on so much she could feel her clitoris throbbing against her labia. Unconsciously she wriggled her bottom from side to side.

Her finger found its target. She pressed it into the little crater, and felt the resistance of his sphincter. The resistance was only momentary. As her finger slipped into his anus he moaned loudly. She felt his cock jerk wildly too. She was going to get her way.

Without changing her rhythm she slid her finger deeper, screwing it into him. She could feel he had passed the point of no return, that this last intrusion was more than he could take. His cock was pulsating, his spunk pumping into it. She felt it swell even more, every vein and contour of it rigid, ready to spit out his seed.

'You're making me come,' he said, his voice low and breathy.

Her finger was completely buried in him now. she twisted it around. As his cock twitched violently she jammed it into the back of her throat. Instantly she felt it kick again and a stream of hot spunk shot out from it, splashing into her throat. Instinctively she found herself suckling on him, wanting to milk him of every last drop of semen, her own body reacting to his ejaculation with a surge of pure pleasure mixed with a feeling of triumph. His spunk tasted sweet. She tried to swallow it all but there was too much. Some dribbled out of her mouth and down her chin.

Gary pulled her head back, his cock slipping out from between her lips. He looked down into her eyes. She could not read his expression. It might have been anger. Or was it lust? Roughly, with undue force, he took her by the shoulders and spun her to one side, so she fell back on the floor, her finger snatched from his rear. In the same instant he fell on top of her, rolling her over on to her back, her dress riding up over her hips. His jeans still around his ankles, he forced her legs open with his thighs and plunged his cock, glistening with her saliva, into her vagina.

Immediately he began to pump it in and out. Once again Clare was taken by surprise. After his orgasm this was the last thing she'd expected him

100

to do. Her surprise increased the impact of his assault. Her body and her mind seemed to close around him, everything narrowing to the compass of her sex, focussed entirely on the feelings it was generating.

He thrust up into her, but he was not as deep as he had been before. Clare could feel he was not as large and not as hard, his cock beginning to soften. He was not stretching her or filling her but that did not stop him hammering into her, the strong muscles of his buttocks powering him forward.

And then the most extraordinary thing happened, something Clare had never experienced before. There, inside her, inside the wetness of her velvety vagina, she felt his penis beginning to grow. As he pounded into her, as her silky wet sex clung to him, just as minutes before her mouth had done, his phallus began to swell. It was the most wonderful feeling, not just physically but because of what it represented. It was the most graphic presentation of desire she could imagine.

Gary stopped thrusting. Instead he jammed his cock as far into her as it would go and let her feel it grow. As it expanded it pushed against the neck of her womb, stretching the soft flesh that enclosed it so tightly.

Clare's body responded with a storm of sensation. She could still taste his spunk in her mouth, still feel the impression his cock had left in her throat, and yet he was inside her sex now, as hard and as big as ever. No man had ever done this, for her and to her. Every nerve was registering that fact. She was completely overwhelmed, emotionally and physically. She was accelerating to orgasm so fast, so furiously, that she hadn't the slightest control. Not that she wanted any. She didn't want anything to get between the waves of pleasure and the effect that they were producing. Her sex was on fire. It had never been so completely filled, so ripe, so replete.

Where before his cock had broken through the secret barrier of her vagina as though battering down a door, now the secret hymen gave way with infinite slowness, pushed back millimetre by millimetre. Ultimately, after what seemed like an eternity, it broke through, his glans surging into the new territory it had found. Or that's what it felt like to Clare. And that's what made her come, a crimson tide of passion simply engulfing her, pulling her down in its undertow.

But that wasn't the end. It was only the beginning. Gary felt her orgasm ringing through her body like the vibrations of a bell. He let it pass, waiting until the last tremor of feeling had taken its toll, then began thrusting forward, his cock as hard as steel, harder, in fact, than it had been before. Her sex, by contrast, was incredibly soft and wet. He dug his hands into her buttocks, using his strength to lift her up towards him, despite her weight and his own.

'Gary, Gary,' Clare moaned. 'What are you doing to me?'

'What you want,' he growled between gritted teeth.

After the climax she had just experienced, Clare could not believe she could take any more. But almost immediately, as the sword of hot flesh stabbed into her, she felt her sex clamping around it, and a new shaft of feeling told her that she was wrong. Her body seemed inexhaustible, insatiable, rapacious. She found her hands were clawing at his small, tight buttocks, urging him on, the feeling of his muscles rippling with effort giving her yet another thrill.

It had never been like this. She was good at sex. She loved sex. She had had good lovers. But it had never been like this. She could come so quickly, so effortlessly. She proved it now, a third orgasm breaking like an enormous tidal wave over his cock.

This time he paid no attention to it. He had his own needs now. He thrust on. On and on and on.

# Chapter Five

'DARLING, HOW ARE you?'

'Overworked and underpaid.'

Clare kissed Angela Barker on both cheeks then pulled herself back up on to the bar stool she had been occupying. Angela wriggled on to one beside her, the fact that this made the short skirt she was wearing reveal even more of her slender, shapely thighs attracting the attention of several men.

'The usual?' Clare asked.

'Please.'

Clare caught the bartender's eye and made a signal to indicate that she wanted another glass identical to the one already sitting on the bar in front of her. Angela had rung her at lunchtime and they'd agreed to meet in their regular haunt, a club tucked away in Bruton Place which was equidistant from Angela's office and Clare's. Angela had said it was urgent.

'So?' Clare asked. 'What's the problem?'

'No problem. Just an opportunity.'

'So what's the opportunity?'

'You know that builder of yours? That hunk.'

Clare looked at Angela steadily, hoping her face gave nothing away. She hadn't told her friend anything about the developments with Gary Newby. 'I didn't realise you were so interested,' she said.

'Come on, he's gorgeous.'

'So?'

The champagne arrived. They both raised their glasses and clinked them together.

'We've got this new photographer. He wants to do a session with non-models. You know the theory, new faces make more of an impact. I think it's a feature on men's suits or something. Well, what's-his-name would be perfect, wouldn't he?'

'I suppose so.'

'Come on, he's got a really good face, and his body . . .'

'Mmm . . .'

There must have been something in her eyes that alerted her friend. 'Hold on a minute,' she said. 'Is there something you haven't told me?'

'Well . . .' Unfortunately Clare found herself blushing.

'You dirty dog – you've fucked him, haven't you?'

The word 'fucked' caused the man at the next bar stool to look around and examine both women carefully.

There was no point in denying it. 'Yes.'

'And?'

'And what?'

'And how was it? I've always fancied a bit of rough trade.'

'Angela!'

'Perhaps I should have my house extended. Come on, give. Let's have all the details.'

'If you want the truth, I don't think I've ever had sex like it.' Clare whispered so the man on the next stool couldn't hear.

'See! I'm definitely going to get my house done. Come on tell me more. Did he have a really wonderful weapon?'

'Angela! Stop it.'

'Only asking.'

'So what about these photographs?' Clare tried to change the subject.

'Do you think he'd do it?'

'I don't know. I'll ask him.'

'You're seeing him again, then?'

'Tomorrow.'

'Get him to give me a ring at the office. What did you say he was called?'

'Gary Newby. Is there any money in it?'

'Of course. I'll go over all that with him. Come on, you've got to tell me more. At least tell me how it happened.'

'I'm not sure.'

'When did it happen?'

'Last Tuesday.'

'And you didn't tell me till now! What happened?'

'He was working late. I offered him a beer. Next thing I know we're in bed together. It was extraordinary. I mean I was just completely swept away.'

'Sounds wonderful. So what else?'

'I'm not going to give you details.'

'And what did you talk about afterwards?' Angela said pointedly. 'You don't exactly have a lot in common, do you?'

'I'm not looking for a husband, Angie. He's a nice guy, I like him.'

'And he's got a big cock?'

Again the man at the next bar stool looked round.

'Stop it. He's taking me out tomorrow night.'

'What, down to the local for a jar and a game of darts?'

'Now who's being a snob?'

'You're not going to let it get serious?'

'It's probably just sex.'

'Probably?'

'OK. Definitely just sex. I know what I'm doing, Angie.'

Clare had been friends with Angela for a long time. They had talked each other through many relationships and, in Angela's case, through a disastrous marriage. However much she would have preferred not to talk about it, what Angela said made sense. It was only a reflection of the thoughts she had had herself. The gulf between her and Gary was enormous and probably unbridgeable if she were looking for a husband. But she wasn't and it didn't stop her having fun with him. Apart from a few one-night stands in her youth (mostly when she had been the worse for alcohol) Clare had always selected her partners on the basis of personality and compatibility. But Gary was different. She had sex with Gary on the basis of a single criterion: her almost overwhelming lust. She had not cared, and still didn't, what sort of man he was, whether he was intelligent, witty, well-read or sociable. All she cared about was getting him into bed. Anything else was a matter of little concern to her. The fact that she had never felt that way about any man before was irrelevant. For once in her life careful planning and deliberation were not going to get her anywhere. If it all ended in tears, as well it might, it would still have been worth it. Of that she was sure.

'And David?' Angela asked. 'Are you going to keep them both?'

'I went down there last weekend. I was going to tell him it was over. Not because of Gary. Just because.'

'And?'

Clare told her about Bridget and her penchant for 'aristos'.

'Well, you've got nothing to feel guilty about, have you? From what you told me he's used you. Now it's your turn to use him.'

Angela's pragmatic attitude to life was refreshing.

'Yes,' Clare said. 'I suppose you're right.'


'What time's your flight?'

'Ten in the morning.'

'And you're sure that's all right?'

'Clare, I'd fly back from New York if it meant meeting a viscount and a duke.'

Bridget was sitting in the boardroom which she had converted into her office for the duration of her stay. Huge blow-ups of all the KissCo display advertisements had been framed and hung around the walls, the eyes, eyebrows, cheeks and lips of various models shaded with KissCo cosmetics and photographs in tight close up.

Clare had learnt that Bridget had decided to fly out to Paris in the morning and was not scheduled to return to London until the following Tuesday. She thought she'd better tell her of David Allston's invitation, feeling sure she would want to change her plans.

'So I'll tell him yes?'

'You bet. Where is this going to be?'

'He's got a really beautiful house in Regent's Park.'

'Great. And this duke?'

'Created 1654 apparently.'

Bridged looked almost stunned at that news. 'Jesus,' she said. 'That's before they discovered America.'

'Not quite.'

'I really appreciate this, Clare. I really do. You and this Viscount Bonmouth, he's slipping you the torpedo, right?'

Clare could have told her to mind her own business. Instead she said, 'Not exactly.'

'Is he married, then?'

'No.'

'What, he's a faggot? A lot of aristos are, I know.'

'I don't think so.'

'So you are having an affair?'

'In a desultory way. Nothing serious.'

'Pity. Jesus, I can't imagine what it's going to be like having dinner with a duke and a viscount.' Bridget's normal steely-eyed intelligence seemed to fly out of the window when it came to contemplating 'aristos'.

'They're only people.'

'No, they're a part of history. Real history.' Suddenly her tone changed. 'So let's talk about Storey and Willis.' Storey and Willis were the advertising agency who'd planned the campaign for the European launch.

'They're good. Very good. They handle a lot of big accounts.'

'Like who?'

Bridget fired off a list of questions. Apparently

the subject of her dinner engagement was closed.

'Hi!'

'Hi!'

He stood outside her front door. It was Wednesday night and he was exactly on time.

'You look great.'

Not sure where she was being taken, Clare had settled for the little black dress. It was silk with a box neckline and a knee-length skirt. She wore very sheer and shiny black tights.

'Thanks. So do you.' She had never seen him in a tie, let alone a suit. The grey suit fitted him perfectly. It made him look older, and no less attractive. Clare's initial response to seeing him again was just as extreme. Her heart was beating so fast it made her breathless. 'Do you want a drink?'

'No.' He said it quickly. Clare sensed he was tempted to come inside but knew if he did they would probably never go out again.

'Shall we take my car?' she asked.

'No, I brought mine. Not the pick-up. Don't worry.'

'I wasn't worried.'

She switched on the burglar alarm and double-locked her front door. He led her to a Ford Mondeo parked a little way up the street. He opened the passenger door for her and closed it after her. As he got behind the wheel he glanced down at her legs, sheathed in the glossy nylon.

'I get this funny feeling when I see you,' he said.

'Like what?'

'Like I want to rape you.'

'It wouldn't be rape, I can tell you that. I feel the

110

same. Do you want to go back to the house?' She half-wished he'd say yes.

'Yes.' But he put the key in the ignition and started the car.

'Where are we going?'

On Sunday morning, after a renewed bout of love-making as energetic as Saturday night, he'd asked her if he could take her out. She'd accepted eagerly, glad of another chance to be with him, but she hadn't questioned him about what they would do and she still had no idea.

'The Key Club. You ever been there?'

'No.' She'd heard of it, though. It was a night-club frequented by the glitterati. The choice surprised her.

'Friend of mine runs it.'

'Really?'

'We were at school together. Lewisham Comprehensive. He's a real high-flier.'

'Sounds like fun.' She wriggled a little uncomfortably in her seat, finding it hard to control an almost irresistible desire to throw herself at him. 'Do you remember my friend Angela?'

'The blonde with the long hair?'

'Yes.'

'She was a bit of all-right,' he said.

'Well she's a journalist. Works for one of those glossy magazines. They're doing a feature of men's fashion and they're looking for new non-professional models. She thought of you.'

'Me!' He laughed. 'What, poncing about on a catwalk?'

'No. Just having your picture taken in some nice clothes.'

'I get to keep the gear?'

'I shouldn't think so, but it pays well.'

111

'Pays money?'

'Absolutely. Are you interested?'

'Yeah. I've never done anything like that before. Beats laying bricks.'

'Here.' She took out a slip of paper from her small, black suede handbag. She'd written out Angela's name, the telephone number of her office and her extension. She tucked it into the breast pocket of his jacket. 'Just ring her up and she'll make all the arrangements.'

'Great.'

He drove quietly, not trying to be macho by speeding or over-taking unnecessarily. They were driving into Knightsbridge past Harvey Nichols.

'Where is this place?' Clare asked. The Key Club had featured in the gossip columns of the tabloids, recalcitrant film or pop stars 'caught' escorting the new man or woman in their life in or out of the premises, but she had no idea where it was.

'Swallow Street, off Piccadilly,' he told her.

They drove down the Hyde Park underpass and found a place to park in Jermyn Street. He ran around to open the passenger door for her. It was a warm evening and there were lots of people roaming the streets, gazing, often wistfully, into the windows of the expensive shops that littered the area.

Gary took her arm and they walked up to Piccadilly. It felt good. Part of the reason she was so sexually attracted to him, she thought, was that he gave off an air of power and physical indestructibility. That made her feel protected. He was tall and broad. Even though she wore her spiky high-heels he was more than a foot taller than her. Both these things made Clare feel especially feminine. In a world where she had broken down the barriers of male dominance, and had paid the price of frequently feeling unfeminine, it was nice to relax back into a more old-fashioned attitude.

There was a queue outside the triangular canvas awning that covered the entrance to the club. Apparently there was no dress code. Men wore anything from T-shirts and jeans to Armani suits; the women an equally diverse gamut of costume, from full-length slinky evening dresses with slingback heels, to satin hot-pants and tank tops with Doc Martens. All were held at bay behind a thick, red, corded rope by two bouncers who looked as though they were refugees from defensive positions in American Football.

Gary walked to the head of the line.

'Good evening, Mr Newby,' one of the bouncers said, smiling and revealing a set of teeth of which a fair proportion had been capped with gold.

'Hi, Harry,' Gary answered cheerily.

The bouncer unclipped the red cordon and allowed them through.

'Evening, Mr Newby.' Inside the swing-doors a pretty redhead sat at a bow-legged gilt table. she was wearing a tight-fitting gold leotard, a keyhold-shaped inset of plain lace cut into the front of the costume. It exposed a great deal of the girl's full cleavage and her flat navel.

'Hi, Betty.'

The girl's eyes examined Clare critically. It wasn't difficult to read her expression. How did anyone get so lucky as to go out with Gary Newby, it said in five-foot-high neon envy.

Gary signed a large leather-bound register, then turned to take Clare's hand.

'Have a nice evening,' Betty said.

This was definitely not what Clare had been expecting. She'd imagined him taking her to some little Italian restaurant in Fulham, not the premier night spot in London. She'd expected him to be hesitant and gauche, not obviously relaxed and at home, and clearly well-known to all the staff. Clare gave herself a metaphorical kick for indulging in unwarranted class distinctions.

They walked through another set of swing-doors. The bar of the Key Club was large and comfortable, and heavily air-conditioned. The arctic blast of chilled air that greeted them was not unwelcome, however, after the heat outside.

'Good evening, Gary.' The *maître d'* stood at a lectern to one side of the door. She was a tall and elegant brunette, wearing a high-cut leotard that was designed to mimic a man's evening dress with a black jacket, a white shirt and a black bow-tie. The woman's long legs were sheathed in black fishnet, the cut of the leotard so high that the crease of her pelvis could be seen under the tights. The garment also necessitated a very severe bikini-line depilation as its crotch was not much thicker than dental floss.

'Hi, Miriam,' Gary said. 'This is Clare Markham.'

'Nice to meet you, Ms Markham,' the woman said, shaking Clare's hand perfunctorily. 'Do you want to have a drink or go straight into dinner?'

'Drink first,' Gary decided.

Miriam turned on her heels and led them over to a corner table, a semi-circular, button-back, red-plush banquette wrapped around a circular table in the American style. There was a white candle floating in a glass bowl in the centre of the table, the water strewn with red rose petals.

114

'Thanks, Miriam,' Gary said, as they squeezed into the banquette. 'Is himself about?'

'He'll be in later,' she replied. She looked at Gary with a smile, and Clare caught, for the briefest of moments, an expression of lust on her face. Then her more professional demeanour returned and she walked back across the bar, her long legs attracting admiring glances from most of the men she passed.

Clare looked round. Beyond the bar was a large restaurant, bustling with waiters. It was decorated in shades of blue, with dark blue walls, a pale blue carpet and a huge display of cornflowers placed on a table in the centre of the room dramatically lit by an overhead spotlight. The rest of the restaurant was dimly lit, with candles flickering on every table, their light reflecting off the sparkling polished glasses and silver cutlery that was set on crisp, starched, white linen tablecloths.

'You like it?' he said.

'Beautifully done. So tell me about your friend?'

A girl in the club uniform of gold leotard with a keyhole-front arrived at the table with an ice bucket containing the stout bulbous bottle of Dom Perignon. She set it down with two tall flutes. 'Compliments of Mr Furness,' she said, expertly opening the champagne without allowing it to pop. She poured an inch of the wine into Gary's glass for him to taste but he dismissed the gesture with a wave of his hand and the girl carefully filled both glasses.

'Cheers,' he said, clinking his glass against Clare's. He looked straight into her eyes, and Clare felt an extraordinary surge of desire. It was a reaction to the longing she saw in his eyes. She

115

wished they had been at home, in her bed, with his naked body ... She shuddered and her nipples stiffened as surely as if they had been touched by a cube of ice. She pulled herself together.

'You said you were at school together?' she said, pursuing the subject of his friend.

'Yeah, that's it. He was always two steps ahead of the game, but we were mates. He used to run all the school dances, stuff like that. We both left school at sixteen and he got a job as roadie to some pop group and he was off. By the time he was twenty he was managing them. They had a couple of big hits. He used the money to buy a club 'cause that's what he always wanted. He sold that a couple of years ago at, like, a mega profit and bought this place. It was on its uppers then.'

'He turned it around?'

'Yeah. And some. He's rolling in it.'

'And you're still friends?'

'Yeah. We still go out for a bevvy. Go to the dogs in Waltham. And the races. And I've helped him re-build his houses.'

'Houses?'

'He's got one in Hampstead, one in Almeria, and a place up here.' He pointed to the ceiling. 'Lets me use them whenever I want. He reckons he's going to buy a place in New York next.'

'A club?'

'No. A flat. That'll be great. I fancy it over there.'

'Were you ever ambitious?' She sipped the champagne. She kept getting the feeling that this was all a waste of precious time. Why were they sitting here making polite small talk when they

116

could have been in bed together, that hard, big cock buried in her soft, melting sex?

'Nah. Not my style. As long as I get my wage packet at the end of the week I'm happy. I don't want any hassle. I'm too lazy. I could never do what Mal does. He works all hours.'

'Mal?'

'My friend. He never stops. I wouldn't want that, not for all the money. Constant worry. Constant stress. All I got to worry about is me mortar going off. Life's too short.'

'I suppose so.'

'And what about you? You've got a good job?'

'Yes.'

'Well then. You must know how Mal feels. Like a treadmill, ain't it?'

'Stop the world, I want to get off? Yes, I suppose it is. But if you don't try you don't get.'

'Right. Don't get me wrong. I like all this. But if I had to really knock myself out to get it, I'd probably not bother.' He smiled, his life laid out before her, its simplicity making her feel slightly envious.

A gold-leotarded waitress arrived with two huge menus, bound in antique leather. She was plumper than most of the other girls and the leotard cut deeply into the soft flesh under her arms and around her buttocks.

'Have anything you want,' Gary said, as if he thought she might be inhibited to order the most expensive things.

They looked over the menu for some minutes, then Miriam was summoned to take their order. 'Your table's ready whenever you are,' she told them, giving Gary yet another generous smile.

'Great,' he said, getting to his feet. 'I'm starving.'

They stood up. As a waitress arrived to take their

glasses and what remained of the champagne over to their table, Miriam escorted them through to the restaurant. Again they were seated at a corner table, where they could survey the rest of the room. Clare spotted a knighted actor having dinner with his wife, and a well-known playwright with a woman who was very definitely not his wife. In fact the scandal of their affair had been all over the papers. Clare knew the photographers would be waiting outside to catch more compromising snaps. Angela had told her how it worked. Waiters at places like this were given a financial incentive to tip off the picture desks of the tabloids whenever a likely couple made an appearance. The restaurants and clubs benefited from the publicity, the papers got their pictures, and the couple in question found themselves in the gossip columns again. Certainly, Clare thought cynically, they would be disappointed if they didn't. There were plenty of restaurants they could go where no one would disturb them.

The service by waiters dressed in black trousers, white shirts and the traditional French, long, linen *tabliers*, was quick and impeccable. They brought the Caesar salad both had ordered almost before the couple had sat down, preparing it on a trolley in front of the table.

'So tell me about you now?' Clare said.

'What you see is what you get.'

'You said you've never been married?'

'No.'

'Anything serious?'

'Yeah, a couple of times.'

'And?'

'I chickened out. What about you?'

'Same.'

118

Gary had the ability to tell her all she needed to know in remarkably few words. With other men she would have quizzed them endlessly about their relationships, wanting to know all the details, but 'I chickened out' seemed to sum up his attitude perfectly. Perhaps it was the fact that their relationship was based on lust and the necessity for anything else had been pared to the bone.

'You're some woman, Clare,' he said. She thought it was the first time he'd used her name. 'I mean you look great.'

'So do you,' she countered. 'You're a very attractive man.'

'Yeah, I've been told. But I'm not in your class.'

'What does that mean?'

'I'm just . . . what did your blonde friend call me? Rough trade?'

Clare thought she might be blushing. She was glad the lights were so low. 'She didn't mean that.'

'Yeah, she did. And it's true. Mind you, I'd prefer to call meself a rough diamond.' He grinned. 'Still don't explain why you're here.'

'Probably pure lust, if you want the truth. Given half the chance I'd tear your clothes off and take you right here in the middle of the restaurant. I'm not sure I've ever felt that way about a man before.'

'Funny,' he said, his grin getting broader. 'I feel exactly the same about you.'

'So you don't think I'm using you to get my hands on your body?'

'Yeah, I do. You ain't going to go out with me for my brain . . .'

They ate their dinner quickly, whether because

they were hungry or because of an unconscious desire to get home neither could say. But Clare, unusually for her, waved away the dessert trolley and settled for a large cappuccino and a small Armagnac.

'Do you want to dance?' he asked. 'There's a disco downstairs.'

'Not really. I want to save my energy.'

A tall, well-built but slightly over-weight man in a white tuxedo and black bow-tie strode across the restaurant towards them. He put his arm around Gary's shoulders and shook his hand vigorously. 'Well, look what the cat's dragged in.' His accent had the same south-London burr as Gary's.

'Clare Markham, this is Malcolm Furness,' Gary said.

'Charmed,' Malcolm said, his eyes giving Clare a none too casual inspection. He shook her hand, rather stiffly. 'Do you mind if I join you?' Without waiting for an answer he grabbed a chair from the adjoining empty table and pulled it up at theirs.

'Gary's told you all about me then, has he? It's all lies,' he said, looking at Clare. He had a podgy round face, with thick jowls and small green eyes. He was bald apart from a horseshoe of hair around his ears and the back of his head, the hair loss making him look a lot older than his friend. Although he was not as handsome physically as Gary there was no doubt that he was an attractive man. He exuded a sort of sexual magnetism Clare was sure a lot of women would respond to. 'Have they looked after you?'

'The food's very good,' Clare said, conscious of her precise vowel sounds in comparison to the two men.

'Well, you're a bit of class, ain't you? Cut above Gary's usual scrubbers. Where did you find her, mate?' He held his hand up to attract a waiter's attention. One scurried over immediately. 'Bring us a bottle of shampoo, Gordon, will you? D–P.'

The waiter hurried away.

'Well now, isn't this cosy.'

'Business good?' Gary asked.

'Excellent. I'm thinking of opening in Madrid. Some guy wants to put up the dosh. Might be fun. You'll have a glass of shampoo, yeah? Before you hit the disco.'

'Actually, we were going home,' Clare said.

'Love it, love it,' Malcolm said clapping his hands. 'I don't think Gary's ever been out with a bird who said "actually".' He was laughing. Oddly it was the same lovely open sound Gary made. Clare was being sent up but it was impossible for her to take offence. 'Well, if you're not going to dance, let me show you somethin' before you go.' Malcolm got to his feet as the waiter brought the champagne. 'Can it,' he told him curtly. 'Come on,' he said. 'Won't take a tick.'

'He wants to show off his pad,' Gary explained. 'Humour him.'

'I'd like to see it,' Clare said, hoping it would not take too long. She had never spent so much time with Gary without sexual contact and her body was beginning to make its frustration felt.

Malcolm led the way across the restaurant and out through a pair of heavy double-doors. In the long corridor beyond they could hear the distant but insistent beat of rock music. They walked down to another set of doors which led to a red, carpeted staircase. At the bottom of the stairs there was another door, heavily padded with quilted red leather.

'This is the main club,' Malcolm explained. 'The bar and restaurant are members only but the disco's open to all. Within reason.'

As he opened the door, the noise hit them like an express train. A cavernous hall was filled with writhing bodies dancing aggressively to loud rock music, shafts of multi-coloured light flickering on and off in time to the tempo of the bass. Around the sides of the room a balcony had been constructed and here the gold-leotarded wait-resses swayed between the tables, carrying trays of exotic-looking cocktails.

Malcolm led them along the edge of the dance floor. At the side of the small stage where two DJs kept the music flowing continuously, he used a key to unlock a small, nondescript door, just behind a bank of speakers mounted on a metal gantry. It opened on to a small corridor, its walls lined with cases of beer and soft drinks. At the end were the stainless steel doors of a lift.

'My private escape route,' he explained, closing the outer door, shutting out at least some of the raucous sound. He pressed the call button of the lift and its door slid open. They crammed inside and Malcolm pressed the single button on the control panel. 'Only one stop,' he said.

They travelled up several floors and arrived at the top with a slight jolt. The doors opened on a small hallway with a single door at one end.

'Home, sweet home. Gary did most of the work by the way,' Malcolm said.

He unlocked the door and stood aside, gesturing for them to go in. Clare found herself in a vast open space, like a New York style 'loft', round steel pillars supporting the ceiling. Three of the walls were stripped brick but the third was made entirely from glass and afforded a panoramic view over London. She hadn't realised they were so far up. She gazed at the vista, the traffic of Piccadilly at the front, with Eros and Piccadilly Circus to the left and the Ritz and Green Park to the right. Beyond that Clare could see Buckingham Palace and the Mall and the tangle of roads that led into Trafalgar Square.

'What a view,' she said, walking over to the glass, mesmerised by the sparkling lights of the city.

'Now we'll have that shampoo,' Malcolm said.

He switched on the lights. Spotlights were carefully arranged on overhead tracks so they lit different areas of the loft separately, creating 'rooms' within the whole. The spotlights illuminated the kitchen, the far corner of the room and another area, in the middle, where four huge and identical sofas were grouped in a square around a large glass coffee table.

Malcolm walked over to the kitchen and took a bottle of Dom Perignon out of a stainless steel fridge the size of a small car. He selected champagne flutes from one of the kitchen cabinets, also fronted in stainless steel, and opened the bottle with a pop.

'I could look at this for hours,' Gary said. He had come to stand next to Clare.

'Can we go home soon?' she whispered.

'Mal's fun,' he said, as if that were a reply.

Malcolm put the glasses and the bottle on the coffee table and slumped on to one of the wild-silk upholstered sofas. He leant forward to pour the wine. 'This is where I come to escape that bleedin' noise.'

123

Clare turned away from the window. Though it was in the furthermost recesses of the room and not lit directly, she could see a large, very low double bed. In the dim light she thought she could make out a figure lying on the ruffled white sheet.

'Well, here's to your taste in women, pal,' Malcolm said, handing Gary and Clare their glasses.

The champagne was delicious, cool and refreshing. Clare sat down next to Gary.

'Honey, you awake?' Malcolm shouted loudly without looking round. 'It's showtime.'

The figure on the bed stirred. It stretched and yawned.

'She's always sleeping,' Malcolm said.

'Hi, honey.' The figure got up from the bed and walked into the light. She was young, probably no more than nineteen, and tall, with raven-black hair so long it hung down her back and brushed over her small but pert buttocks. Her face was long, with high cheek-bones, a large, sensual mouth and big, dark-brown eyes. She was naked apart from a pair of tiny black panties, no more than a triangle of shiny silk attached to thin black straps. Her breasts were small, like inverted saucers, but her nipples were as big as doorknobs and each was surrounded by wide, dark areolae.

'Say hello to everyone,' Malcolm said.

'Hi, guys,' she said. Her accent was American. She walked over to the sofas and curled herself up next to Malcolm.

'This is Liza,' he said.

'I'm Liza,' she agreed.

'I pick up a lot of strays in my job,' Malcolm said, looking at Clare. 'I saved this one from a white-slaver, didn't I, honey?'

'You sure did.'

'A what?' Clare said in astonishment.

'She was being shipped out to Africa.'

'Are you serious?' Clare asked.

'Yeah. Perfectly. In this business you see a lot of it. She was working downstairs. These guys promised to get her a job as a dancer – that's what she is, a dancer . . .'

'Dancer,' Liza agreed sleepily.

'They gave her a one-way ticket to Cairo. Well a couple of my girls went the same way. Never came back. Never seen again, so I knew these guys.'

'He saved me.' The girl sat up. She picked up a glass of champagne and drank half of it. 'My saviour,' she said, running her hand up Malcolm's thighs until it reached his crotch.

'You see how grateful she is?'

'You're such a jammy sod,' Gary said.

'I think we should go now.' Clare touched Gary's arm.

'No, don't go,' Liza said with feeling. 'I love to dance.' She jumped to her feet, her lethargy gone. There was a hi-fi stacked in a black metal frame over against one of the steel pillars. She ran over to it and turned it on, a haunting saxophone filled the air, as it played the melody of 'My Funny Valentine'.

Almost before Clare realised what was going to happen the American had cleared the coffee table of glasses and jumped on to it, her body swaying to the music. Sensually she ran her hands down the sides of her body, then back up again, over her navel and her petite breasts. She squeezed and kneaded the scant curves. Her long black hair swung across her back, as she swayed her head in time to the music.

Clare's reaction was unequivocal. If anyone had asked her ten minutes ago what she would feel about watching a semi-naked girl performing an exotic dance three feet in front of her eyes she would have replied that the idea had no appeal. But she couldn't have been more wrong about her reaction. The lithe body of the girl and the sinuous movements she was making with it were hypnotic. She couldn't tear her eyes away from her. What's more she felt her pulse racing.

'Lovely little mover,' Malcolm said. He was stripping off his jacket and bow-tie, and unbuttoning his shirt.

The American brought her hands over her cinched, narrow waist and hooked her thumbs into the thin black straps that held the triangle of her panties in place. Bringing her knees together she turned so her buttocks were facing Clare, then slowly inched the black silk over her hips and down her legs. Clare saw the long slit of her sex emerge. It was pursed between her thighs, the labia completely hairless. With the black silk at her knees, she raised herself off the glass and stripped the panties away.

Gary slid his hand on to Clare's thigh. She tore her eyes away from the girl to look at him. His eyes were seeking her assurance that she wanted to stay. He found it, Clare's excitement obviously written in her face. He smiled, then turned back to the spectacle on the glass table.

The girl, kneeling on all fours now, spread her thighs apart. Clare watched as her right arm was pushed through between her legs and began to caress her buttocks, her hips swaying from side to side in time to the music, her head hanging down so her long hair brushed the glass. She spread the

126

cheeks of her buttocks apart so Clare had a clear view of her anus, a little wrinkled crater, and her smooth, rather thin labia. Gradually working lower the fingers parted the folds of her sex deliberately exposing the crimson mouth of her vagina. It was wet and glistened under the bright spotlights.

Still in the same position, Liza drove one finger deep into her sex. She gave a little mew of pleasure then withdrew it, added a second finger and plunged them both back in. Taking both out, she bunched together three fingers and pushed them into her sex, their combined breadth stretching her labia around them.

Clare felt each penetration as though it were in her own body, each producing a stab of sexual excitement. She tried to suppress a moan but wasn't sure she succeeded. Gary's hand had worked its way up under her skirt and was clutching at her thigh, and she saw Malcolm glancing, casually, at the flesh he had exposed, then he looked up into her face and their eyes met. He smiled and she wondered if he could see her arousal.

In a graceful, balletic movement, the American slowly removed her fingers from her vagina, then lay flat out on her stomach, twisting around so she faced Malcolm. She inched herself towards him, sinuously like a snake, her generously curved buttocks swaying from side to side.

Malcolm shifted to the edge of the sofa. Liza reached forward and took hold of his knees, using them to lever her face up between his thighs, her body forming a bridge between the table and the sofa. Clare saw Malcolm's hand disappear under her head and a moment later caught a glimpse of

127

his erect penis, before Liza gobbled it into her mouth.

At exactly that moment Gary's finger pressed up between Clare's legs. With the unerring accuracy he had demonstrated before, he pressed the sheer nylon of her tights into her labia, and found her clitoris, rubbing it delicately up and down. Clare felt a surge of pleasure. Her whole body shuddered. She hadn't realised how much Liza's performance had affected her. But Gary's finger was tapping into a source of sexual energy that had already been created. She told herself women were not supposed to be aroused by voyeuristic pleasures, especially involving other women, but it appeared patently obvious that she had been.

Clare had never thought of herself as particularly moralistic or conventional, but a strong, puritanical streak was struggling to assert itself. It was telling her that she should get up and walk out. She had never been in the same room with a couple in the throes of sex. She had seen porno movies – though she found them of limited appeal – but had never, in real life, seen what Liza was doing to Malcolm or, for that matter, allowed anyone to see what Gary was doing to her. This was turning in to an orgy and the voice in her head was telling her that, like her last experience with David Allston, it was going too far. But with David she had felt disgust and distaste. Here, now, she felt no such thing. If she were honest with herself, at the deepest level, all she felt was an overwhelming sense of exhilaration. Buried deep in her sexual psyche, there was also another strand of arousal caused by all this, that gave a new edge to her feelings, but which, as yet, she could not properly identify.

Gary's finger was relentless as she watched the brunette pull her head back from Malcolm's cock, then plunge down on it again. Malcolm was looking straight at Clare, his eyes focussed on her legs.

With the agility of an acrobat Liza pulled her mouth off Malcolm's erection, rolled over on her back and jack-knifed her legs into the air. She seemed to somersault over the gap between the edge of the table and Malcolm's knees and land squarely in his lap facing outward, his erection sticking up from her loins, as if she had sprouted a penis.

Clare stared at his cock. It was wet from Liza's saliva, broad and gnarled with large, prominent veins, its foreskin still partially covering the glans. As she watched, Liza took it in her hand and jerked his foreskin back, circling the newly exposed glans with her thumb and forefinger. It throbbed visibly and Malcolm moaned. The American raised herself on her haunches and guided the cock into her thin labia. With no hair to obstruct the view, Clare could see it disappear as the girl sunk down again.

Gary got to his feet. He stripped off his jacket. there was a huge bulge tenting the front of his trousers. He kicked off his shoes and socks and pulled down his trousers and boxer shorts. His erection sprung free.

'Lovely,' Liza said.

'What do you want me to do?' Clare asked. She needed help. She had never been in a situation like this before. It all felt unbelievably wicked and more wanton than anything she had ever done before, but the element of the forbidden, of breaking taboos, the fact that she knew she

129

shouldn't be doing this, only served to increase her excitement. It was too late to turn back now, much too late.

Without saying a word Gary took her by the shoulders, pushed her over on to her side then rolled her on to her stomach. Taking her by the hips his strong arms pulled her up to her knees, facing along the length of the couch. Climbing up on to the seat behind her, he pulled the skirt of the dress up roughly. She felt his cock nudging against her nylon-covered buttocks, then pull back as his hands grabbed the waistband of the tights and pulled them down until they banded her thighs.

Liza had begun to bounce up and down in Malcolm's lap. Clare could see his erection sliding in and out of her, slicked with her juices. He had wrapped his arm around her body and his fingers were pulling at her big, fat nipples. Each inward thrust of Malcolm's penis into the obviously wet depths of Liza's vagina made Clare's sex clench in sympathy. Malcolm's hands had cupped Liza's breasts, and continued to pluck at her nipples. That in turn, made Clare's nipples pulse. Nestling in her black lace bra, they were puckered and hard, their arousal so extreme they seemed to be pulling at the flesh of her breasts, stretching it as taut as a drumskin.

Gary's hands were circling her buttocks, pushing her dress up to her waist, then caressing the bare curves. She could feel the heat of his cock. He gripped her by the hips and pulled her backwards towards him, the top of his glans parting her labia as it nosed into her vagina.

Clare's body experienced another shock of pleasure. Gary had made no attempt to thrust up inside her, and yet the sensations his cock created was almost as great as if he had. There were theories, she knew, about chemical reactions between some men and women. That was the only way she could explain the effect he had on her. She had had good sex before. Very good sex. But never anything like this. Sexual exhilaration flowed through her body like an electric current.

Gary lent forward. She felt his hand slide around her body and into her lap, delving into the bunched-up tights until it found the apex of her thighs. Her labia were already stretched apart by the breadth of his erection, and her clitoris was exposed. It was so swollen he found it instantly, pressing it back against her pubic bone then pushing it up and down as he had been doing before. It was exactly what Clare wanted. But then Gary always seemed to know what she wanted.

Her clitoris reacted to this new onslaught with a pulsating burst of sensation. She felt her sex purse around his glans. Since she had known Gary she didn't think she had ever orgasmed so quickly or with such consummate ease. The ability to manipulate and control the feelings that lanced through her, which she had used so effectively in the past, had simply disappeared. There was nothing she could do but allow herself to be swept along by the flow. And that's what was happening now. As Gary's finger moved against her engorged clitoris, dragging it up and down, Clare's body lurched into gear, the sensations of pleasure coming in waves, an orgasm already in play.

'Please,' she said, wriggling her buttocks against him, trying to show him how much she needed deeper penetration.

'Pretty please,' he said. His other hand reached

forward to her neck, pulling her head back until it was almost at right angles to her spine, then caressing the taut sinews of her throat. With her head up Clare found herself staring at Liza's naked body and Malcolm's cock, thrusting rhythmically into it. The sight only accelerated her passion, rushing her towards orgasm.

Exactly at the right moment, as if he were so attuned to her feelings her body had given him some secret signal, Gary plunged his cock forward with all his strength. Clare couldn't tell whether she'd come the second before this invasion or the second after it. But whichever it was, the feeling of his cock filling her again so completely created a new intensity, pushing her to limits of pleasure that tested anything she'd felt before. Her body went rigid, every muscle clenched, every tendon stretched, her mind blank but for a curtain of crimson that oscillated in time to the frequency of her pleasure.

It took a long time for her to regain her senses. Her orgasm had been so sudden and so intense it had wiped out her memory, like a deep sleep sometimes could. For a moment she was not sure where she was or what she was doing. She shook her head, trying to clear it. Liza and Malcolm had stopped moving and were both looking at her. She registered their presence with a shock, then discovered it was a pleasant one.

Clare was strangely calm, almost detached. She knew exactly what she wanted. And she had every intention of getting it. Her orgasm had put her in touch with her feelings, with that hidden, secret strand of sexuality she had not been able to identify. She knew what it was now.

Slowly she rocked forward on her knees. Gary's

cock popped out of her, a disjunction that caused her to shudder. But it did not divert her from her aim. Getting to her feet she kicked off her shoes and stripped the tights the rest of the way down her legs. Gary looked puzzled, unable to read the expression on her face.

Clare unzipped the black silk dress, slipped it down over her shoulders and wriggled it over her hips. She stepped out of it then threw it on to one of the sofas. She was naked now but for her black lace bra. She saw Liza's eyes looking at her body, and Malcolm doing the same, his head peering around the brunette. Slowly she reached behind her back with both hands and unhooked the clip of the bra. Then, like an expert stripper, she used one hand to hold the cups against her breasts while the other slipped the thin shoulder straps over her arms.

She had never behaved like this before. She had never done anything so blatant but she knew precisely why she was doing it now. The look of lust in Malcolm's eyes, and the fact that she knew Gary behind her would be equally inflamed by the sight of her naked body, was tremendously exciting. But that was not what affected her most.

Liza was brunette whereas Andrea had been blonde but there was something about her, something that, unconsciously, Clare had obviously recognised from the moment she had climbed up on to the coffee table, something that had stirred memories of her childhood friend. Perhaps it was her long, lithe body. Perhaps it was her eyes, and the way she'd looked at Clare. Perhaps it was the way she moved so sensually. Or none of those things, just the fact that for only the second time in her life, she had found herself staring at the naked body of another woman, displayed overtly for her benefit.

Whatever it was, it had jolted a powerful source of sexual excitement. Clare had kept that memory hidden away, not shamefully, because she felt no shame. It was just a secret, her secret. A secret she had shared with no one else, the wonderful pleasure she'd experienced that June afternoon on her birthday, something she could not forget. Fortunately it hadn't got in the way of her relationships with men; in fact it only served to enhance them, teaching her how strongly her body could respond in the right circumstances.

Andrea had never tried to touch her again after that. They had remained good friends but the experience was never repeated. Since that time Clare had never had another lesbian encounter, nor had felt the slightest desire for one. Until now. Now those particular floodgates seemed to have opened and a tidal wave of lust was carrying her along. She didn't want to work out why – that would have been fruitless. She knew she would never have the faintest idea. She couldn't have worked out how she knew Liza was open to such an approach either, but knew it for a fact.

Clare let the bra fall away from her breasts. They quivered at their sudden freedom. She cupped them in her hands and squeezed them hard, so their nipples stuck out more prominently. Then she took a step forward, hooked her hand around Liza's neck and stooped to kiss her on the mouth. As she had known she would, Liza kissed back eagerly, her tongue dancing against Clare's.

The first impact was marked. Clare hadn't

kissed a woman for so long she had completely forgotten what it felt like. She was astonished at the difference from kissing a man. The mouth was softer, more pliant, melting against hers.

'Well, look at that,' Malcolm said, looking at Gary.

Clare took Liza's hand and pulled her to her feet, Malcolm's cock disengaging with a plop. As the American stood up Clare embraced her, crushing their bodies together and feeling a new wave of passion. She was sure the girl would not reject her advances, but if there had been any lingering doubt it disappeared as she felt the way the girl writhed in her arms, responding with clear enthusiasm. She could feel the hardness of her big nipples pressing in to her own breasts, and the girl's thigh levering up between her legs until it was rubbing against her wet labia.

They didn't say anything to each other. There was no need. Both were high, primed by the men. Both had the same desires, perfectly matched. As though with practised ease they slid on to the sofa next to Malcolm, laying out full length on it, while their tongues and mouths remained locked, their bodies undulating subtly, responding to a rhythm that was buried in each of them, the beginning of a circle that could have only one end.

As Clare had taken the initiative, she continued to make the pace. Breaking away from Liza's mouth she licked and nibbled her way down to the girl's long neck, over her chest to her nipples. Breathlessly, her heart thumping against her ribs, she sucked the left nipple into her mouth, pinching it between her teeth, making the girl gasp. She transferred her mouth to the right and produced an identical effect.

'Oh yes, yes, that's what I want,' Liza cried, stretching out on the sofa, her arms above her head, one foot slipping to the floor so her thighs were open and her sex exposed.

Clare's excitement was intense. She licked her way over the girl's belly, the thoughts of Andrea, of that hot birthday afternoon adding to her arousal. She was out of control, she knew, and it didn't matter. Nothing mattered to her but her desire. Her tongue explored the American's belly button, making her arch her buttocks off the sofa, then dipped down between her legs, her mouth crushed against the girl's hairless, thin labia. A surge of sensation seized both women simultaneously. They both moaned, though Clare's exclamation was gagged on Liza's sex.

'Together,' the American said urgently. 'Both of us.'

There was no need to explain what that meant. It was what Clare wanted too. Feeling that strange calm that had gripped her minutes before, she got to her feet. Liza's body lay supine stretched taut by her need.

For a long moment Clare stood there, knowing both men were watching her, acutely aware of their eyes on her naked body and waiting for her next move. Liza looked up at her too, those big brown eyes pleading with her to finish what she had so unexpectedly begun.

And that is what she did. With her pulse racing, she knelt on the sofa and swung her thigh over the girl's shoulders, so her sex was poised above her head. Then she leant forward and, for the second time, pressed her lips into the brunette's hairless sex, lowering herself on her haunches so the girl could do the same thing to her. She had known how it would thrill her. But the anticipation was a pale imitation of the actual event. As the circle closed, a charge of pure pleasure shot through them both, at the same time. A line had been thrown back into the past and, as Liza's tongue, hot and wet, delved into her labia to find her clitoris, the past was reeled in, the intervening years fading away, the memory sharpening until it was crystal clear, a direct connection made between then and now, the one feeding off the other.

Their bodies were joined, their mouths and sexes connected, completing a circuit, their feelings, like an electric current looping around a cooper coil, charged up to a higher voltage. Every sensation provoked an equal and opposite response, the feeling of Liza's tongue artfully circling Clare's clitoris, somehow expanded by the fact Clare was doing exactly the same thing to her. There were so many different sensations it was impossible to keep track of them all. But, over-riding everything, Clare's mind was caught up in a maelstrom of images, memories of Andrea's body inevitably intermingled with the reality of how Liza's felt. Clare had deliberately stopped herself from using the memory as an icon of sexual pleasure. But now it was out, now she had given in to it, the potency of its effect on her was marked, expanding her consciousness of everything she felt.

Clare was coming. Clare was sure she'd come the moment their sexes had been locked on to their mouths, but everything was so exaggerated now, and so extreme, that her earlier orgasm seemed like nothing in comparison to the one that accelerated through her now. Everything she did to Liza, and everything Liza did to her, every touch, every caress, every delicate movement of tongue and clitoris was amplified in their vortex of feelings. So it seemed were their orgasms, their bodies perfectly in tune, every wave of pleasure mirrored and matched in the other, their mutual climax approaching rapidly.

Who came first it was impossible to tell. By that time they were barely divisible, their two bodies united into one, a writhing mass of flesh, heaving, sweating, gasping for air with the same urgency and passion, clinging to each other for support, knowing exactly what the other felt.

Clare hadn't really recovered when she felt hands pulling at her shoulders. She was only vaguely aware of being peeled off Liza and carried, bodily, over to the other sofa. The first thing that shocked her out of her enervated state was the sudden intrusion of a large, hard, throbbing phallus, burying itself in her soaking-wet sex.

She opened her eyes. Gary was poised above her, looking down into her face. His eyes were alight, wild with lust. He began pounding his cock into her, thrusting it as deep as it would go, his balls banging against her labia like two battering rams. For a moment Clare felt her body swoon, literally overwhelmed by sensation, unable to cope. But that did not last for long. Sharp, almost painful feelings took hold of her. Suddenly she wanted more. In fact, she wanted more very much and more of what Gary was so comprehensively giving her.

She glanced over at Liza and saw Malcolm positioned above her too, her legs wrapped around his back, his buttocks pummelling up and down.

'This what you want,' Gary said between gritted

teeth. It was not a question. His cock was twitching violently. What he'd seen had fuelled his need. His cock was always hard and hot but she had never felt it like this before. Despite the massive spending she had already had, she knew she would come again just as powerfully. She watched with fascination as Malcolm pounded into Liza. It was a mirror image of what was happening to her, being able to see what Gary was doing to her from a different perspective as well as feel it. The image excited her but then everything excited her. She felt Gary's cock swell and knew he was going to come. She knew also with absolute certainty that his ejaculation would provoke her again, as it always had, her seeming indefatigable body already on the brink of a mind-racking, nerve-jangling orgasm.

# Chapter Six

*AT EIGHT THIRTY* the next morning Clare's phone rang, waking her from a deep and apparently dreamless sleep. It was Bridget Goldsmith.

'Look Clare, I'm sorry to ask you to do this but I need you to come to Paris this morning. We've got to go over some problems with Claude.'

'Fine. It's an hour ahead, right? I suppose I can be there by midday.' Her mind had snapped into gear.

'Come straight to the office. We'll be waiting.'

'Fine.'

Clare rolled out of bed and into the bath. In fifteen minutes she was dressed in a smart, lightweight grey suit. She drove her car to the airport, left it in the short-term car park and bought a club-class ticket to Paris on the first available flight.

There was a thirty-minute wait. In the lounge she dialled her secretary's home number on her mobile phone and told her of the change of plans, asking her to call the French office and arrange for a car to meet her flight.

She called Gary's home. She hoped he'd be free tonight. She badly wanted to see him again, and tell him that what had happened last night had changed nothing as far as she was concerned. There was no reply. She tried his mobile. That, the operator told her, was switched off.

Fortunately the flight was on time. It landed in Paris at ten to eleven, which was ten to twelve French time. A large black Citroën was waiting for her. Thirty minutes later she was sitting in the offices of KissCo on the rue St Honoré.

Claude Duhamel was a chunky man, with wild, bushy eyebrows and thick, wiry hair. He did not like Clare. She did not like him. Both knew that, in all likelihood, after the European launch KissCo would rearrange their European operations and one of them would be left running a distribution organisation with no responsibility for marketing. That amounted to a serious demotion.

Claude had picked up on Clare's declared strategy for advertising. Perhaps seeing that Bridget approved of the idea of using the commercials already running in America, instead of making costly new ones for each country in the EC, he had strongly objected to Clare's plan.

After an hour's discussion, with Clare's research on previous campaigns where American commercials had been used and achieved a deeply negative impact faxed over from London, they adjourned for lunch at Lasserre. A small lift took them to the first-floor dining room where, as Paris was hotter than London, the electrically-operated roof had been retracted, the whole room beautifully cool and light. The gourmet food was all but ignored, the battle raging between the two

141

points of view, with Bridget taking a far from impartial stand.

Nothing was resolved. They continued the discussion back at rue St Honoré.

'Well, I guess it's going to be up to me to decide,' Bridget said finally. As usual she was wearing white, a trouser suit with narrow, quite tight-fitting trousers, and a jacket that buttoned up to the collar-bone, under which she wore no blouse. Her chestnut hair was tied into a rather severe chignon that made her look distinctly older, despite the fact her face was remarkably unlined. A big gold brooch, shaped like an Egyptian scareb, was pinned over her left breast.

'In the end,' Claude said, wanting to have the last word, 'it comes down to money. Re-making the commercials would be a gigantic waste of money.'

'I couldn't agree less,' Clare said.

'You've made your views clear,' Bridget told her.

'They are not just views. They are backed up by reams of evidence.'

'The examples you are using are not for cosmetics,' Claude said. 'They are entirely different products. The analogy is false.'

The argument was going round in circles, getting nowhere.

'So, let's leave it there. It's my job to decide.' Bridget smiled. 'The buck stops here. If you don't mind, Clare, I'm going to fly back to London with you.'

'Of course,' Clare said, though she did not relish the idea. It had already been a long day after a late night and she was tired. Sitting next to

Bridget on the plane would not be restful. Shop talk would continue.

'I hope you will think very seriously about what I have said,' Claude interposed. 'Not just about the advertising.'

'Give me the weekend. Then I'll let you know.'

The black Citroën took them back to Charles de Gaulle and they walked straight on to the next flight back to London.

'I wanted to ask you about tomorrow night,' Bridget said as they refused the club-class stewardess's offer of a glass of champagne, and opted for orange juice instead.

For a moment Clare's mind went blank. 'Tomorrow night?'

'The dinner, Viscount Bonmouth . . .'

'Oh, right.' She'd forgotten all about David. Last night had wiped that slate clean.

'I was wondering what I should wear. Will it be very formal?'

'Formal?' Clare had an image of Bridget dressed to the nines in ermine and pearls, with long, white, lace gloves and a tiara.

'You know, evening dresses?'

'I shouldn't think so. Do you want me to ask?'

'Would you? I'd hate to turn up in a cocktail dress when everyone else is in ball gowns. Do aristos dress for dinner?'

'They don't in the country.'

'No. But this is in town and he did say there's going to be a duke there. How do I address a duke?'

'Your Grace, I think.'

'Jesus. Really? Your Grace?'

'I'll give David a ring.'

'Would you? I haven't got a long dress with me so I'd have to go get one.'

'I'll ring him now if you like.' There was an airphone built into the seat in front of them.

'Perfect. Just got to go to the powder-room.'

As Bridget made her way down the aisle Clare took out her address book and dialled David's number. There was no reply from the London house and the butler in the country told her that David would be out until seven. She left a message for him to call her, then dialled Gary's mobile phone.

'Hello?'

'Gary, it's Clare.'

'Hi.' The line was a little echoey, a slight delay in the time the signal took to bounce off the geo-stationary satellite.

'I had to fly to Paris, sorry.'

'Where are you now?'

'In the plane on the way back.'

'So how are you?'

'Busy.'

'I didn't mean that.'

'If you mean physically, I'm sore.' She lowered her voice. 'Deliciously sore.'

'Yeah, I bet. You shouldn't have been so greedy.'

'You make me greedy.'

'Where does it hurt, exactly?'

'You should know.'

'I tried to phone you earlier.'

'At the office?' She'd given him all her numbers.

'Yeah. I got your secretary. I thought you were a secretary.'

Clare wasn't sure whether he was joking. They

144

had never talked about her job. 'I'm a very important cog in a very unimportant wheel,' she said, a little defensively.

'What are you doing tonight?'

'Nothing. Can I see you?'

'You're not too tired?'

'Are you?'

'I'm fine.'

'Come around to my house when you've finished.'

'I'm knocking down a chimney. I'm covered in soot.'

'I can wash your back.' And your front, she thought to herself, her sex suddenly reminding her of its existence with a strong pulse of feeling.

'Yeah? I might like that.'

Bridget Goldsmith slid back into the seat beside her.

'So might I. I'll be back about seven.'

'It's a deal.'

They exchanged goodbyes. As she put the phone back in its housing Clare realised her hand was trembling.'

'He was out,' she explained. 'I've left a message.'

'Call me at the hotel, would you? I might have to go shopping in the morning.'

She unlocked her front door at six forty-five. Wanting to stay alert after her late night, Clare had not had a drink all day. But now she needed one. She went into her new kitchen. The tilers had finished the walls and floor on Wednesday, and apart from a little painting scheduled for tomorrow the extension was finished. It looked good but, unless she had managed to convince

Bridget Goldsmith of the efficacy of her plans, it would be her last extravagance for some time. Bonus-related pay was not a feature of running a distribution depot.

Opening a bottle of champagne, she took it through to the sitting room and slumped on to one of the sofas. The wine was too cold but that was refreshing.

She was just thinking about going upstairs to shower when the phone rang. As it was exactly seven o'clock she knew it would be David.

'Clare? Hello, darling, I got your message. I had to come up to town. I was going to ring you anyway.'

'Really? You go first then.'

'I just wondered what you were doing tonight. I've been out on one of my little shopping expeditions.'

'Oh.' Clare's heart sank. She knew what that was code for. More gold-foil-wrapped parcels. Worse, it meant David had not picked up on her disgust at their last encounter. She supposed it was possible that he could have taken her departure from the script as an excess of excitement, that she had finally begun to express her own regime of fantasies. She cursed Bridget Goldsmith. If it wasn't for her she could have told him the truth.

'I thought perhaps you might like to write the letter this time. I have to tell you, darling, what you did, it was wonderful. I've been thinking about it. You know I'm very stuck in my ways. I was a bit miffed at first. But, well, the more I thought about what you did the more I thought it was just amazing.'

'The trouble is . . .' She tried to think of an excuse.

'It would be a nice prelude to tomorrow night. Tomorrow night's special too. I think you'll be surprised.'

'You haven't forgotten I've invited Bridget?'

'No, no, of course not. I know that's important to you. But after dinner. Well, let's just say after last Friday I think you'll be very pleasantly surprised.'

'Look, David, I can't make tonight. I've just got too much work to get through. I've been in Paris all day. You know what it's like with Bridget here.'

'Oh.' The disappointment in his voice was obvious. He had geared himself up for another erotic interlude, an outfit for Clare no doubt waiting to be gift-wrapped. What would it be this time? A cheap red suspender belt with ruched black suspenders, and fishnet stockings, or incredibly expensive couture creations in silk as soft as the nap of a peach? Clare didn't care. She didn't want any part of it.

'I tried to ring you last night,' he said. She could hear from his voice he was pouting like a child whose favourite toy had just been taken away.

'I was working late.'

'I tried the office. They said you'd gone home.'

'I told them to say that, David. I didn't want to be disturbed.'

'Oh, pity. There's nothing wrong, is there?'

'No,' she lied. 'Look, Bridget asked me to find out what she should wear. I think she's got the idea that ermine and tiaras are statutory with members of the British aristocracy.'

'It's black tie for the men. Something slinky and long would be nice.'

'I'll tell her.'

'What about you, what are you going to wear?'

'Any preferences?'

147

'Red. You know I love you in red.'

'I don't have a long red dress.'

'I wasn't talking about your dress.'

'David!' She mimed shock.

'You remember that tight, red body I bought you. The satin one with the lace insets and the suspenders. You could wear that. And if you're wearing a long skirt you could wear stockings too.' She could hear his voice getting more breathy. 'I love to think of you sitting at dinner all prim and proper when I know what you're wearing underneath. You're so gorgeous, Clare.'

She remembered the red body. It was a silky satin, woven with Lycra so it clung to her like a second skin. The lace insets were positioned so as to veil her breasts and her lower belly.

'I'll think about it,' she said.

'I don't see why I can't see you tonight,' he said moodily.

'Please, David.'

'You could make it up to me.'

'I have got work to do.'

'What are you wearing now?' That was another piece of code. They had played this game before. It always started with the same question.

Clare sighed. If today had shown her anything at all it was how tight Bridget's decision about the European launch was likely to be. Claude's arguments had been so close to Bridget's view that Clare needed any edge she could get, and David's dinner party was a very definite trump card. If it were cancelled things might look bleak.

'Where do you want me to start?' she asked wearily. She sipped her champagne to fortify herself.

'Shoes.'

'Black. Patent leather. Very shiny. Very high heels,' she said.

'Very shiny?'

'Yes.'

'Tights or stockings?' His voice was thin and reedy.

'Stockings, of course.'

'What sort?'

'Fifteen denier, Very sheer. Very glossy. Midnight blue, with thick tops, very thick and dark.'

'Skirt or dress?'

'Skirt. A short skirt. Too short really. Too short for stockings. One of those stretchy ones. Clings to my bum.' She heard a sharp intake of breath.

'Colour?'

'Red.'

'Blouse?'

'White. Too tight over my tits. Satin.'

'A white blouse?' He sounded puzzled, as though something were wrong.

'Yes.'

His voice stuttered as he said, 'Bra?'

'Black. I know I shouldn't wear black under white. It shows. Everyone can see it.' She knew for some reason that especially excited him.

'What sort of bra?' His voice was becoming increasingly strangulated.

'Underwired lace cup with a plunge front.' It didn't take much imagination to guess what he was doing. Descriptions of female clothes always seemed to excite him, the more tarty the outfit the better. She imagined him standing in his bedroom by the phone, his erection in his hand.

'What sort of material?'

'Lace.'

'Pushes your tits together.'

149

'Up and together. Quite a cleavage.'

'Such lovely tits. Are you wearing a suspender belt?'

'Yes. Black too. Very thin.'

'Satin?'

She could hear him panting slightly. 'Yes, with a lace frill.'

'And panties?'

'Yes.'

'Black?'

'Naturally.'

'What kind of panties?'

The conversation was coming to an end. Like a lot of David's rituals he liked it to end in the same way. She had to remember what was required of her. At least, she thought, this was better than spending the night with him.

'French knickers,' she replied on cue.

'Satin and lace?'

'Yes.'

'Black satin and lace.' He said it with a sort of reverence in his voice.

Her next line was always the same. 'Like the sort I like to see you wear, David.'

'No!' He cried in mock horror.

'Yes.'

'Got to go now,' he said.

'Mmm . . . so have I,' she added as suggestively as she could. The line went dead.

'I told you I was filthy.'

He stood in the hall. His hair was so caked in dust it stood on end and his face was encrusted with grime apart from white patches around his eyes where he'd obviously been wearing goggles. His T-shirt and jeans were so dirty they would have stood up on their own.

'Fortunately I have a brand new bathroom, with a brand new bath and newly-tiled surrounds,' she said, grinning and trying to resist the temptation to throw him to the floor and rip his trousers off. It wasn't easy.

'They've finished, then? Grouting dry?'

'They did it on Wednesday.'

'Should be all right, then.'

'You can christen the bath. I've only used the shower so far.'

'Great.'

There was always a slight uneasiness between them on first meeting, she thought, or perhaps it was just that her overwhelming desire for him made it difficult to concentrate on anything else.

'Go on up, you know the way. I've opened a bottle of champagne.'

'Can I have a beer first to wash the dust away?'

'You can have anything you want.'

He took her arm just as she was about to turn away and looked into her eyes fiercely. 'You, all right?'

'Fine,' she said with a sparkle, wanting him to see she bore no scars.

'Good,' he said, releasing her. He climbed the stairs, taking the steps two at a time.

As Clare opened his beer, pouring it into a glass this time, she heard the water running in the new bathroom overhead. She was glad it had been such a full day at work. It had given her no time to dwell on the events of last night, or her reaction to them. The truth was she felt not one iota of regret and she had no intention of developing it out of some false sense of morality. Certainly what had happened was beyond anything she'd experienced before.

Certainly she had no desire to make a habit of it. But in terms of pure hedonistic pleasure she could never remember having had such a good time.

Clare had always been careful. She had not exactly measured out her life in coffee spoons, but she had dealt with sex as methodically and intelligently as she had dealt with all the other aspects of her life. She had never allowed herself to act on impulse. Until Gary, that is.

Gary's sexual charisma affected Clare in two ways. It had affected her physically. The orgasms he had induced in her at the drop of a proverbial hat had been shattering. She had always considered herself a good lover, good for her partner and good for herself, adept and sexually aware of her own body's needs; but what Gary did to her was something quite other. It made her feel that her previous sexual experience had been too studied and controlled – controlled by her. With Gary she was completely out of control and had been from the very first time, bending over the bath in what she would call, from now on, the old bathroom. She had not been conscious of doing anything, of making calculations as to what was or was not the best thing to do. Her body had responded at the most primitive level. Even the thought of what they had done created a response she had never experienced before, her nipples hardening, her sex becoming moist and prickly as surely as if it were a conditioned reflex to a physical stimulus.

But her extraordinary receptiveness to Gary had spilled over into other areas. It seemed to have swept away all her inhibitions. Admittedly, David Allston's sex-games had tested the frontiers of what Clare had thought of as acceptable, but his elaborate fantasies had been as nothing compared to the situation she had found herself in last night. And it was her response to that situation that had surprised her. As little as a week ago she knew, without the slightest doubt, she would have walked – not to say run – out of Malcolm Furness's 'loft' the moment Liza began to slither her tiny black panties down her long slender thighs. Instead her reaction had been total fascination. Just as Gary's sexual prowess had overwhelmed her physically, it had affected her mentally too, allowing her to listen to the wilder side of her nature – to respond, she supposed it was fair to say, more honestly, without the circumspection she usually imposed on all her actions.

The same motivation accounted for her reaction to Liza. It had been an experiment but one she had undertaken due to the new responsiveness Gary had inspired, the ability to react at a purely instinctive level. Not only had the experiment been a success in terms of her physical pleasure; it had released, like a genie from a bottle, the spectre of Andrea, a spectre that had haunted her for years. However hard she had hidden the experience from herself, because she had no idea how to cope with it, she had never been able to forget what had happened and the ghost could not be laid to rest. The excitement she had felt in Liza's arms, the feelings the girl had given her and she had returned in equal measure, and the powerful orgasm they had shared, had made Clare realise quite simply that she had nothing to be afraid of from the memory of what had happened with Andrea. The pleasure had been unequivocal. It had also been, more importantly, under her control. She didn't imagine she would want to repeat the experience of being with a woman again, but if she did, if another moment arose, she would not fear it, as she had after Andrea. Before she had feared that lesbianism was like a sort of virus that she might catch and keep. Now she knew it was just another sexual experience, another means of arousal, with no implications or consequences for her future sexual orientation.

She collected her champagne glass from the front room and went upstairs. The bathroom door was closed.

'Can I come in?' she asked, feeling a little foolish.

'Yeah. Nothing you ain't seen already.'

She opened the door. Gary was lying up to his neck in bubbles in her new white bath. He grinned.

'This is great,' he said, as she handed him the beer and sat on the edge of the bath. She hadn't had time to change and still wore the skirt of her business suit and a white blouse. 'You gonna get in too?'

That sounded like a good idea. 'Mmm. I think I will.'

She stood up and undid her blouse, suddenly feeling a little self-conscious. Apart from last night, when circumstances were far from normal, she'd never really undressed for him. They had rarely made love naked, their passion being so great their clothes had to be merely torn aside. She was wearing a pink jacquard bra. She unzipped her skirt and stepped out of it. Inevitably, it seemed, her pulse quickened.

'You have an extraordinary effect on me,' she told him. She pulled her flesh coloured tights

154

down. Her matching pink panties had high-cut legs trimmed with lace.

'Nice arse,' he said. The triangular back of the panties was stretched tightly over her buttocks. She could see it in the mirror that had been so recently fitted behind the length of the bath.

'Glad you think so,' she said, trying to be casual about unclipping and discarding her bra.

'Nice tits, too.'

'Thank you, kind sir,' she mocked, sliding her panties down her legs.'

'You're not very hairy down there,' he said, looking at her pubes.

'No. Never have been. Do you mind?'

She stepped into the opposite end of the bath and sunk down into the water, stretching her legs out on either side of his body, glad for the moment of the protection of the mountain of bubbles, and congratulating herself on deciding on such a large bath tub.

'No, I like it.' He raised his leg and pushed his foot up against her crotch, wriggling his toes. 'You were really in the mood last night, weren't you?'

'I surprised myself,' she said, trying not to blush. She raised her leg, swung it over his thigh, and planted her foot against his cock. Her display had evoked the right response. He was already erect, his phallus only just submerged under the surface of the water. She pushed the sole of her foot against it.

'See what you do to me,' he said.

'You're very responsive.'

'So what? You into women too? It was quite a show.'

'Let's just say it was a one-off.' She didn't want

to tell Gary about Andrea. She had never told anyone about that. 'And what about you? Was it a one-off for you? Or does Malcolm often invite you up there for a little party?'

Gary grinned. 'Malcolm's a bad boy. I often think the only reason he went into nightclubs was so he could have wall-to-wall tarts.'

'You didn't answer my question.' She pushed her foot against his cock even harder, pressing it back on to his navel. She felt it twitch.

'We've had a few nights up there. He can usually conjure up a couple of dollies to do the business.'

'Like last night?'

'Don't do any harm. You enjoyed yourself, didn't you?'

'I thought that was obvious.'

'I've never been out with a bird like you.'

'Fucked or dated?' Clare asked pointedly.

Gary laughed. 'See. Real smart. Dated, then. Some of Mal's birds were classy little pieces.'

'Is that what I am?'

'Yeah. Posh. Educated. Smart.'

'Does it make any difference?'

'Not to me. It does to you, though.'

'Does it?'

'It makes things a lot easier.'

'Easier?'

'Yeah. With me you get what you see. A bit of a laugh and a good fuck. No complications. No problems.'

'What sort of problems?'

He pushed his big toe between her labia. The water had washed away all the natural lubrication she knew she had been producing since he walked into her house, and her sex felt a bit dry.

156

'You know. If I was like you – I mean if I was some bloke with a degree and a plum in his mouth with his rabbit, and a good job behind some desk . . .'

'What?'

'Well then you'd immediately be thinking that was it. You know. Marriage. Kids and the like. With me you ain't got none of that.'

'Don't I?'

'Oh come on, love. No point pretending. This ain't ever going to go anywhere. A bit of a laugh and a good seeing-to. That's it. End of story.'

Clare looked at him. He was smiling, the corner of his eyes wrinkled up by his amusement. She thought he was probably the most beautiful man she'd ever seen in her life. Almost unconsciously she wriggled her bottom so her clitoris butted up against his toe. He was right, of course, completely right. There was no point pretending. Realistically, though she hadn't thought it through, there was no long-term future in their relationship. They had nothing in common apart from sex. That didn't mean, in the short term, they didn't have a very healthy mutual interest in each other. There was something very freeing about being involved with a man for such narrow reasons, no actions held to account at a later date, no worries about what might or might not go wrong.

'And what if I told you I was in love with you?' she asked coquettishly.

'You're not. And you won't be.'

'I'm in lust with you.'

'Yeah. Great, ain't it?' He moved his foot. Miraculously his big toe found the opening to her vagina. It had been sealed by the water, dry and

157

unyielding, but he pushed forward until the seal broke. Beyond, where the water had not penetrated, was a well of hot, sticky juices.

Clare moaned. 'So what's going to happen?'

'You'll get bored or I'll get bored.'

'As simple as that.'

'Life's too bleedin' complicated as it is without making it worse.'

It was Clare's turn to laugh. Gary's total lack of ambition, his contentment with his lot and his reluctance to allow emotional complications to disturb practical considerations were deeply rooted in his personality. His feet were planted firmly on the ground and no 'tart' was going to change that, certainly not one with a plum in her mouth and a good job.

'This is the first time we haven't just thrown ourselves at each other,' she said.

'I had my protection on. Dust and baked-on sweat.'

'But now you're all squeaky clean . . .' She rubbed the sole of her foot up and down his cock. 'I want to show you something,' she said, having an idea. She got to her feet, the water running from her body, his toe unplugged from her sex. Drying herself perfunctorily on one of the big fluffy bath towels that were draped over the new towel rail, she marched into the bedroom through the doorway Gary had built.

'So what's all this?' he asked, coming out of the bathroom with a towel in his hand, his erection sticking out in front of him.

'This,' she said. She stripped off the counterpane and lay on her back on the white undersheet. Twisting around to her bedside table she opened the drawer and extracted her vibrator.

'I want you to watch.'

Gary looked puzzled. He was standing at the foot of the bed. Clare stretched her left leg over to him and touched her foot against his knee, then spread both her legs wide apart. She pushed the tip of the dildo down between her labia, until it was resting against her clitoris, and then switched it on, the hum of its vibrations filling the air.

Gary's eyes locked on her sex. She used her spare hand to squeeze at her right breast. 'Mmm . . . feels good,' she said, undulating her hips.

'Do you do this a lot?' he asked. His erection seemed to be pointing directly at her.

'What, use the vibrator or let men see me doing it?'

'Both.'

'I use the vibrator a lot.' She raised her buttocks off the bed, slid the tip of the vibrator down her labia and then pushed it into her vagina. Very slowly she let him see it disappearing into her sex. The look in his eyes excited her. Her sex was thoroughly wet now. As she drew the vibrator out she knew it would be slicked with her juices. 'But I'm very particular about who I let watch,' she said.

'Christ, look at that,' he said as the dildo slid back up, her labia pursed around it.

The vibrations began to affect her. She groaned as the dildo filled her, the strong oscillations somehow matched to the frequency of pleasure already coursing through her body. The dildo was not a substitute for that big, thick cock she could see right in front of her, but she was excited by what she was doing and the way she had got Gary to stare at her so intently.

'I get hungry, you see,' she said, sawing the dildo in and out more rapidly.

Gary's fist circled his cock. He held it tightly, making the protruding glans swell.

Clare pulled the dildo right out of her vagina and centred it on her clitoris again. The sudden concentration of vibrations on the little nub of nerves produced a wave of pleasure that made her roll her eyes closed.

'You bitch,' he said, with no venom in his voice. 'You little bitch.'

She opened her eyes again. Gary wasn't looking at her sex now. He was staring into her face as if all this contained a meaning he was struggling to understand. After last night she couldn't believe he was shocked, but that would have been one way to read his expression. Then, almost as quickly as it had appeared, the shadow of doubt, or concern, or whatever it was, evaporated. He was not good at being passive. He was a doer, not a watcher.

Clare supposed, at least unconsciously, that what happened next was what she'd been trying to provoke. In one fluid movement Gary sprung forward, took hold of both Clare's wrists, stretched them out above her head, pinioning her by them, his lean, muscular body pressing down on top of her. His rock-hard erection slipped between her legs. Raising his hips he guided his glans into her labia, forcing them apart just as the dildo had done.

'Oh Gary.' The contrast with the dildo was marked. It had been cold and inanimate. His cock was hot and large and pulsing with life.

He stretched her arms out above her head until her sinews were taut. He opened his legs using his ankles to spread her legs further apart too, spread-eagling her flat across the bed, his cock at the centre of the X their bodies formed. He raised his hips so he was arched up over her, and only the tip of his cock was touching her clitoris. Then he jerked his cock, making it move against her. That was enough to make her shudder, her sex contracting like a fish gasping for air.

'Let me have it,' she begged.

'What do you want? Me or that thing?'

'You, of course.' She was confused. He couldn't possibly imagine she preferred the dildo to him.

He stayed as he was, his body rigid, poised above her, all his strength concentrated on spreading her limbs apart. His cock brushed her clitoris with an infuriating lightness of touch.

'*Please.*'

She had never wanted him so much. She could feel every inch of her empty vagina and every inch of it wanted to be filled by him. It was a void, an aching void, needing him to make it complete. She tried to raise her head, to struggle up but with no arms to use for leverage she made little impression on his iron grip. The feeling of his body, of his sinewy, corded muscle gave her need another cruel twist.

'Please!' she said, her tone angry not begging.

Suddenly, with almost brutal force, his body collapsed on top of her, his legs scissored together, his cock driving up into her so forcefully his pelvis hammered against her labia. As she had always felt with him, the meat of his cock filled her completely, causing a sensation of pure pleasure so strong she could do nothing but wallow in it. Her sex recovered quickly, wrapping itself around the intruder in a convulsive spasm, clinging tightly to every inch of the hard, unyielding flesh.

Clare thought she could wrestle herself back

under control after the initial impact, and she could have done, had Gary pulled out of her, even slightly. But he did not. Instead, his body as rigid as a board, he focussed his energy on forcing his phallus even deeper into her, his glans pressing up against the neck of her womb. His strength was such that as he arched his body like a bow, his arms straight and supporting his weight, he was actually dragging her off the bed too, her sex hooked on his cock.

She had never felt him so deep, nor his body so taut. She wrapped her arms around his back, and pushed herself down on him, wanting what he wanted, her senses reeling, her orgasm breaking like a wave over the hardness impaled inside her. She rolled her head from side to side, making a peculiar baying sound she had never heard herself make before, her orgasm radiating out from her sex. It did not fade. Like a thunderstorm caught in a valley, it came round again, each streak of lightning no more or less intense than the last, each clap of thunder making her whole body tremble and quake.

It went on forever. It was still rolling through her body when she felt him relax back on the bed, his grip on her limbs slackening, his buttocks starting to rise and fall, plunging his cock in and out like a piston rod. It didn't take long for this new strategy to affect her as much as the old. As he pumped into her, each forward thrust creating that strange illusion of breaking through that secret barrier in her sex, her nerves girded themselves for another onslaught.

Her hands raked his back. She dug her fingers into his buttocks, wanting to feel his pounding muscles. He turned his head and kissed her hard on the mouth, thrusting his tongue between her lips, its heat a match for the heat of his cock, an electrical connection established between the two, using her body as its helpless conduit. Again she was propelled into a heady orgasm, or was it just the same one, extended and intensified until it felt like something new? She didn't know or care.

'Oh Gary, Gary, what are you doing to me?'

He didn't stop. He hammered on. Perhaps he felt she was not finished, sensed that she could come again. Or perhaps it was his own need that drove him forward so relentlessly, all the way in and practically all the way out, the base of his shaft grinding against her clitoris on the inward stroke. Whatever the motivation she came yet again, a sharp, almost painful shock of pleasure emanating from her beleaguered clitoris, completely different from the last two orgasms and yet essentially the same.

Gary stopped. He pulled out of her and rolled to one side.

'Turn over,' he ordered.

'Can't,' she muttered. It was true. Her body wouldn't respond.

He took hold of her and turned her over on to her stomach. Kneeling behind her, he took hold of her hips and pulled her up to her knees, just as he had last night on Malcolm Furness's sofa. He looked around for the vibrator.

The feeling of his hot, sticky cock nestling itself into the cleft of her buttocks revived her.

'Aren't you going to come?'

'Yes,' he replied.

Every time Gary had come inside her before it had made her come again. But this time she was not so sure it would have the same effect. After last night and what he'd done to her already this evening, she felt as though she were satiated. She couldn't have been more wrong.

His hands held her buttocks. He was spreading them apart, looking down at her reddened labia, and the little, perfectly circular hole of her anus. A lot of Clare's juices had run down between her legs and the cleft of her buttocks were wet. Slowly he pressed his glans against the corrugated flesh.

Clare knew at once what he intended. 'No,' she said sharply.

'Yes,' he insisted.

'Gary, I can't.' She felt a shudder of fear. Men had tried to have anal sex with her before. She had always refused them. The trouble was she didn't want to refuse Gary. 'I've never done it,' she told him.

'I want it,' he said quietly.

The desire in his voice excited her. The single most exciting thing about Gary was probably the fact that he so self-evidently desired her so much. The fear Clare felt transmogrified into something more complex. Whatever else she was feeling, Clare's lethargy had disappeared.

'Be gentle,' she said.

He pressed forward. She felt the little ring of muscles resist. For an instant she had the desire to pull away, yet she held her nerve. She knew there was bound to be pain, but everything Gary had done to her before had brought her tremendous pleasure so she was prepared to believe that this would too. She tried to relax.

'Try,' he said.

She made a conscious effort. He felt her body give way. He pressed forward and watched as his

164

glans sank into her.

Clare felt a shock of pain that took her breath away. Her body tensed again, all her nerves screaming in protest. But almost immediately the wave of pain was translated into a surge of pleasure, a sort of pleasure that, even bearing in mind the extremes she had experienced in the last few days, she had never felt before. It was a pleasure on the same wavelength as pain and of the same incredible intensity, one barely distinguishable from the other.

Clare braced herself again. Gary had hardly penetrated her at all and he was readying himself for a second thrust.

'Love it,' he said. His hands grasped her hips. The wetness of her juices had lubricated his cock. He thrust forward hard, the breadth of him stretching her, his excitement all the greater for knowing he was the first to do this to her. His cock slid deeper, then, with another push, as deep as it would go.

Clare gasped. Another wave of pain rushed through her but this time she knew what to expect. Just as instantly as before, the pain mutated to quite extraordinary pleasure, wave upon wave of it. And then, among all the feelings that invaded her, in the mass of new sensations that having a big hard cock buried in her rear for the first time, produced in her, she felt another burgeoning emotion: relief. Her fear had been unjustified. There was pain but it was far outweighed by swelling, orchestrated pleasure.

Tentatively she pushed back against him. His cock twitched inside her. She seemed to be able to feel every inch of it, the smoothness of his glans and the ridge underneath it, though she was sure that was just her imagination playing tricks in her over-heated mind. The pain was now no more than a tingle of discomfort, and that was overlaid with a flood of passion. It was good. She had never thought it would be but it was wonderfully sexy. She wriggled her bum from side to side and experienced a whole new range of thrills.

Gary leant forward. She felt his hand snake under her belly. Something hard pressed up into her labia. It found the opening of her vagina and was inside her before she realised what it was. He'd found the vibrator and used it to invade her sex. Her whole body heaved, the two phalluses buried inside her, divided only by the thin membranes of her body. So much of what Gary had done to her was like nothing she'd ever experienced before, in extent if not in fact. But this was both. Not only had she never had anal sex, she had never had two phalluses inside her at the same time. Her rear passage seemed to be able to deliver pleasure with as great an impact as her vagina. Gary's cock had filled her but this feeling doubled that sensation. Her body had never been so stretched, her nerves hardly able to cope with the intensity of it all. There was nothing else. The only reality was the two phalluses and the two passages of her body that clung to them, and her clitoris pulsating wildly.

Just as she thought she could feel no more, more came. Gary turned the control of the vibrator and its familiar vibrations began to pummel at her. As quickly as if someone had flicked a switch Clare felt herself coming, a huge current of sensation, a tidal wave of passion, about to break over her.

But there was more. The vibrator imparted its

166

oscillations to Gary's cock, as they were pressed so closely together. The two vibrated in harmony but Gary's cock also began to jerk forcefully against the tight confines that imprisoned it. Each tiny kick provided Clare with a rush of euphoria. She could feel it swelling too and knew he was going to come.

That realisation hit Clare at exactly the same moment as her orgasm. Milliseconds later, as the waves of thick, super-heated pleasure coursed through her she felt his cock swell for the last time. Pleasure turned to pain momentarily as it stretched her untrained rear to its limits. but the pain was twisted back into pleasure in time for her to feel his ejaculation. She would have sworn she could feel every spurt of it, as it splattered into her, where no man had come before. Each jet produced a spasm of gratification that made her whole body shake, the vibrations of the dildo elongating each until, by some alchemy, a new pleasure was wrought, like the effect of fire on metal, a white-hot passion that burnt everything it touched.

Both were exhausted. The dildo slipped from her body long before his cock softened and slid out too.

They lay side by side, alone and yet together, their bodies touching, but with no energy left to feel the contact.

# *Chapter Seven*

---

*HE STAYED FOR* breakfast. He told her he liked to start the day with bacon and eggs so she ran to the corner shop and bought bacon because she had none in the house. She gave him orange juice and coffee and a mountain of wholemeal toast which he spread with strawberry jam, telling her he preferred marmalade.

He sat in her new kitchen, which was big enough for a kitchen table, in her white towelling robe, its arms too short for him, its shoulders barely containing his broad back.

'What are you doing tonight?' he asked as he finished off the last piece of toast.

'Dinner. Business dinner.' It was half true.

'Oh.'

She was delighted that he looked disappointed. Though they had quite sensibly agreed there was no future in their relationship and that their motives were purely carnal, she was glad he wanted to exercise his carnal desires at every opportunity.

'So what about Saturday?' she suggested.

'I was going to tell you about that.'

'Go on.'

'You know that photo-shoot you told me about.'

*Photo-shoot*. That sounded as if he'd been talking to Angela. 'Yes.'

'Well, it's tomorrow afternoon. Angie said it might go on most of the night. They want to do some night shots, apparently.'

'You got it, then. Why didn't you tell me before?'

'We got sort of busy.'

'What happened?'

'Angie sent this photographer guy round to the site. He took a couple of shots on Polaroid. Then Angie called me on my mobile to say I was on. Good, eh?'

'Very. How much are they paying you?'

'A thousand if they publish. Five hundred if not.'

'Not bad.'

'Money for old rope.'

'I could come and watch.'

'Can you do that?'

'I go to most of our campaign shoots.'

'What sort of campaigns?'

'Cosmetics. That's what KissCo does.'

'Right KissCo. That's what the girl said on the switchboard when I called your office. They do all those big billboards with the girl with hairy eyebrows and the huge mouth.'

'The bigger the mouth the more lipstick. Anyway, that's what I do.'

'What?'

'Run KissCo UK.'

'No wonder you've got a bleedin' BMW.'

'Company car. Look, I'll ring Angie. She can

give me all the details. Then we can have dinner afterwards.'

'If that's all right.'

'I'll arrange it. Angie won't mind.'

'Christ,' he said, looking at his watch. 'I've got to go.'

He finished his coffee and dashed upstairs. A few minutes later he was in her hall in the dirty jeans and T-shirt he'd arrived in last night. At the front door he gathered her into his big arms and kissed her hard on the mouth, squeezing her to him. She felt his cock stir against her belly and wished they could have kept the world at bay for a few more hours.

'Angie?'

'Clare, darling, how are you?'

'Fine. I gather you've got yourself a new model?' Clare had waited until she was at work to call her friend.

'Who told you that? Oh, of course, I forgot. Pillow talk.'

'So tell me all.'

'Jeff went around to see him. You know what Jeff's like, he gets the hots for anything that looks as though it's real. He went ape. Brought back some snaps. Margy said yes. The rest is history.'

'You're shooting tomorrow?'

'Afternoon and evening.'

'So I gather. Is a thousand the going-rate?'

'Now why should that interest you?'

'He's a friend, Angie.'

'A friend. Come on, Clare, it's me you're talking to.'

'I just want to make sure he gets the going-rate.'

'A thousand's fair. Take my word for it.'

'Good. So can I come along?'

'What?'

'Can I come and watch the shoot?'

'Ah . . . no.' Angela's voice was hesitant.

'No? Why not?'

'Clare, do I have to spell it out for you?'

'Yes.'

'We're going to feature Stickshift.'

'So?' Stickshift was the fastest growing competitor to KissCo, a Spanish company backed by German money that was pouring millions of pounds into a slick marketing campaign that suggested wearing their cosmetics would produce instant sexual gratification. The phallic connotations of the company's name, based on the American word for a manual gear lever, featured heavily to establish a sub-conscious psychological connection between their products and the results they could induce.

'Come on, Clare, you know it's not possible. You wouldn't have Conchita Martinez at one of your shoots.'

'No, but I thought this was about men's suits?'

'It is. Was. But Margy's done a deal with Stickshift to split the costs. Girls are going to be pouting their lips all over your lover-boy.'

'I could come in disguise.'

'Clare, I'd get shot.'

She knew Angie was right. If anyone from Stickshift was near one of KissCo's photographic sessions, Clare would blow a fuse.

'All right. Just take care of him, then.'

'I will. He's safe in my hands. Trust me.'

'I wouldn't trust you as far as I could throw you, which with your weight problem, isn't very far.'

'You're only jealous of my tits.'

'True. Have fun.'

Bridget had hired a chauffeur-driven Daimler for the duration of her stay and it had been decided that they should travel together in it to David Allston's house.

As usual Bridget was wearing white – a white chiffon top with full sleeves over a tight, strapless dress that clung to her body as though it had been painted on. The designer of the dress had layered a large chevron in a shade of off-white over the front of the dress, its apex reaching down to mid-thigh as if to draw attention to the fact that from this point the full-length skirt was split all the way up from the ankles. The split revealed a great deal of Bridget's long legs, sheathed in sheer, white nylon. Her white suede shoes were emblazoned with a gold crescent-moon.

Clare's outfit was less revealing. The last thing she wanted to do was tantalise David Allston. She had chosen a rather severe crêpe dress in burgundy, with long sleeves and a full skirt. Only the sweetheart neckline revealed a hint of flesh, but no more than a hint, the neckline not low enough to expose much of her cleavage.

The chauffeur double-parked the Daimler outside the Nash house and raced around to open the rear passenger door for them. A dark-green Rolls Royce was parked behind David's burgundy-coloured Bentley, its chauffeur already asleep behind the wheel, his cap pulled down over his face.

They walked up to the front door. Clare rang the bell. She was expecting the butler to answer but it was David Allston himself who opened the door.

'Hello there,' he said cheerily, stepping forward to kiss Clare on both cheeks.

'This is Bridget Goldsmith, David Allston,' she said.

'Or, if you prefer, the Viscount Bonmouth,' he added, seeing Clare had missed the opportunity and wanting to impress her boss.

'I'm so pleased to meet you, my Lord.' Bridget had looked the form of address up in the office copy of Debrett's. She curtsied and then shook his hand.

'Actually, I really do prefer "David". Come in. Come in.'

'This is some house,' Bridget said, as she stepped into the vestibule.

'Been in the family for two hundred years. Nash, of course. He designed the whole lay-out of Regent's Park and Regent Street. I don't know if you knew that. Wonderful man. Unusually for the eighteenth century he lived to see the whole scheme completed. Most of them popped off before they were fifty.'

'Is that so?' Bridget said, staring at David as though he were a godlike figure.

'Come through. Come through. You're interested in history, Clare tells me.'

'We have so little of it in the States.'

David led the way into the large sitting room. there were four other guests all standing by a large fireplace, the grate filled with a display of dried flowers.

'Let me try and introduce you,' David said. 'Not very good with names. This is Bridget . . .'

'Goldsmith,' Bridget prompted.

'Right. Bridget Goldsmith, a visitor from America, and my dear friend Clare Markham.'

The four guests nodded and smiled. 'This is Virginia Ansel,' he said, indicating a large divaesque woman in a voluminous blue velvet dress. 'Her friend Anna Holmes.' He gestured towards a waif-like girl with long but stringy blonde hair who wore a yellow satin and lace creation that did nothing to hide the fact she was painfully thin. 'And Philip and Celeste Richardson, the Duke and Duchess of Tidmouth.'

Bridget and Clare shook hands with the guests as they were introduced. When Bridget got to the Duke she curtsied and bowed her head sharply. 'Your Grace,' she said solemnly.

'Let me get you both a drink,' David said.

Clare was surprised that there were no servants. It appeared that the guests were helping themselves to champagne, several bottles of which had been dug into a pile of ice in a large round silver bowl standing on a mahogany side-table. David picked out one of the bottles and poured the wine into two long thin flutes.

Bridget's attention was riveted on the Duke. He was a small, slightly plump but comparatively young man with thick, lank black hair and very dark brown eyes that gave the impression of a certain beadiness, but which were examining every contour of Bridget's figure quite overtly, apparently oblivious to his wife who stood at his elbow. Celeste Richardson was tall, taller than her husband, and Clare guessed older, her dark auburn hair pinned up to her head, her rather long face etched with lines, her green eyes large and bright. she had an air of detachment about her, as though she were watching everything at one remove. Of all the women her dress was the most spectacular, a black-and-white print, boned, grosgrain corset-style with a full, pleated, chiffon, black skirt.

'Can I have a word?' David asked Bridget. He looked at his other guests. 'I think we're all agreed, aren't we?' he said to them. They in turn all nodded or mumbled 'yes'.

'What is all this?' Bridget wondered.

'I haven't the faintest idea,' Clare said. She hoped it wasn't one of David's little games. She'd thought she made it clear enough that her career was on the line with this woman.

'Please let me explain,' David said. He took her arm and led her over to the window that over-looked the park.

'David's told us so much about you,' Virginia Ansel said.

'We know all your secrets,' the Duke added.

Clare wasn't paying that much attention. She was trying to read the expression on Bridget's face. At the moment it looked like puzzlement.

'Have you known him long?' she asked Virginia.

'We joined two years ago.'

'Joined?' Clare thought that was an odd word to use.

'The Society of Oser,' Celeste said.

'What?'

'David's little jokes. You know what he's like,' the Duke said.

*Oser* was French for 'to dare'. A cold hand gripped Clare's heart but she saw the expression on Bridget's face change from puzzlement to what was quite obviously delight. David leant forward, his face only inches from her ear.

'It's only Anna's third time,' Virginia said.

'More's the pity. Didn't know what I was missing.'

175

'What is this Society?' Clare said.

'Oh.' The Duke said looking at his wife uneasily. 'He hasn't told you? We thought . . .'

'I'm sure David knows what he's doing, darling,' Celeste said quickly. 'Would you like some more champagne?'

'No, thank you.'

David led Bridget back to the little gaggle of guests. Whatever else was going on Clare was glad to see her boss was beaming with delight.

'So are you going to tell me all about your family, your Grace,' she said to the Duke. 'I'm really fascinated.'

As Philip launched into an explanation as to the origins of the dukedom, David took Clare's arm. 'I really appreciate you coming tonight, Clare, I want you to know that,' he said with such an intensity it was obvious he wasn't just talking about dinner.

'What is all this?' Clare asked. 'What's going on here? Where are the servants?'

'Their night off. Don't worry, there's a beautiful buffet. Everything's arranged.'

'And the Society of Oser?'

He took her by the arm and led her into a corner. 'Don't worry. I've explained it all to Bridget. She's a surprisingly sophisticated woman. We don't usually invite singles but I explained to the others and they all agreed once they'd seen her . . .'

'Explained what?' Clare was becoming increasingly confused and annoyed. What was there to explain about a dinner party?

'What happened between us, Clare, at the house last time,' he continued, ignoring her question. 'It was difficult for you, I know.'

'I have to talk to you about that.'

'I know. I know. It was all too sudden. But I

knew you'd understand. I knew I could trust you, Clare. You are such an amazing woman. What you did . . .'

'I couldn't help my reaction.'

'That's the point, isn't it? I knew then. I knew it would be all right. I know I've been very demanding. I know my sex-life is a bit of a maze.'

'To put it mildly.'

'Yes. As you say, to put it mildly.' He was looking straight into her eyes as if trying to see into her soul. 'I know what happened. That's what made it so exciting for me. It was the first time, the first time you got involved; the first time you thought about yourself and not just about me. God, it was wonderful, Clare. I haven't been able to stop thinking about it. That's why I had to phone you. The way you looked. The expression on your face. Your voice. So strong. So imperious. And what you made me do. Oh darling, I know that's just the beginning.'

Clare had been right. She guessed yesterday he had completely misconstrued her reactions to what had happened. He'd used the fact that she had not kept to his script as evidence for her excitement, not as an indication of her disgust.

'Look, David, we need to talk,' she said emphatically.

'Yes, yes, of course. I know what you are going to say. No more letters. No more scripts. We don't need that now. What you did on Friday was better than anything I could have made up. We are on the same wavelength now, I know.'

With Bridget ten feet away on the other side of the room this was not the time to tell him the truth, Clare decided.

'That's the point,' he said. 'That's why I wanted

177

you to come tonight. Then you'll see everything.'

'Everything?'

'It's a question of finding a way to express yourself. Finding a way to express what you need. That's the point, isn't it? I feel so foolish. I've been stifling your expression. You've been so unselfish, so giving, it never occurred to me to ask what you wanted. But here you can do whatever you please, you can take whatever you want to take. And I can show you what I really am, Clare. No more half truths.'

'David, I really don't think this is the place.'

'No. You're wrong. Everyone here is the same.'

'The same?'

'I'd never have dared ask you here before. But now. Now I know it's what you want too, even if you haven't properly realised it yet.'

None of this was making any sense to Clare. 'What have you got planned?' she said with a sinking heart.

'You'll see.'

'And you've invited Bridget to join in?'

'A remarkable woman.'

'What if she'd refused? Did you think about that? This was supposed to be a dinner party.' Whatever else was going on, dinner was clearly very low on the agenda.

'We would have had our buffet very sedately then wished her goodnight. But she said she knew the moment she walked into the room. The Americans are very instinctive, aren't they?'

'Knew what?'

'Something in the eyes, she said.' He turned around to the other guests and said, in a loud voice, 'Ladies and gentleman, as my butler would say, dinner is served.'

The guests all appeared to know where to go. They filed through a door at the back of the sitting room into a large dining room, its walls decorated with a collection of Chinese Imari plates. The vast mahogany dining table had been laid with what the Victorians called a cold collation. There was a whole salmon in aspic, a glass bowl full of crevettes – their tails hanging over its edge, several dozen oysters, plates of salami and cold meats, as well as potato, tomato, green and pasta salads. There were silver sauce boats filled with mayonnaise, cocktail sauce, and vinaigrette dressing, and baskets full of a variety of different breads. At the far end were a selection of desserts, glazed strawberry and raspberry tarts, a concoction of meringue and chocolate, and a huge mound of profiteroles as well as a crystal bowl of fresh fruit salad. Several bottles of red and white wine had been opened and stood next to sparkling solid silver cutlery, white crockery, crystal glasses and starched linen napkins on a separate table near the door.

The guests ploughed into the food unceremoniously. After her conversation with David, Clare was not feeling hungry but watched as Bridget sliced herself a piece of salmon and spooned tomato salad on to her plate.

'How's the Duke?' Clare asked her, walking over to her.

'He's a charming guy. Real cute. Never dream he was a duke if you saw him on the street.'

'David talked to you, right?'

'Sure. I knew as soon as I walked in the door. Did he tell you that?'

'Yes.' She wanted to ask what she knew but couldn't think of a way to put it without making

179

herself seem incredibly naive.

'Mind you, I'd never have guessed you'd be into it. Don't worry though, honey. I'm not prejudiced. It ain't going to affect your prospects. Well, that would be hypocritical, right? To tell you the truth, there's a little group in Houston I join when I'm in the mood.'

The conversation only succeeded in confusing Clare further. She hadn't the faintest idea what David or Bridget was talking about. She felt like Alice who had just stepped through the looking-glass into a world she did not understand. All that was important to her at the moment, however, was that Bridget seemed to have taken whatever was going on in her stride.

Bridget resumed her dialogue with the Duke as soon as he had collected his food. Clare took some salad and picked at it unenthusiastically, watching as David joined the conversation with her boss. For a while she stood alone, watching the guests devouring the food, their appetites keen, apart from the blonde, who went straight to the fruit salad and ate nothing else.

'Bridget's your boss, isn't she?' Celeste asked, coming to stand at her side.

'Yes.'

'She's an attractive woman.' The Duchess was staring at Bridget openly, her eyes roaming the American's body.

'I suppose so.'

'So are you, of course. Very. It's always fun, isn't it? Imagining.'

'Imagining?'

'Perhaps that's the wrong word. Anticipating would be better.'

'Anticipating what?'

The woman had a small mouth with very thin lips. Clare saw the tip of her tongue lick her upper lip.

'Anticipating what I would do with Bridget, for example. Or you. I'm not sure which prospect excites me most.'

'Ladies and gentleman.' David's voice interrupted her musings. 'I think it's time to get on with the proceedings. As you know, we have a guest amongst us tonight but she has agreed to participate. When you've all finished supper we will begin.'

There was a little smattering of applause as David walked out of the room, pausing only to smile, a little nervously, at Clare.

'What's going on now?' Clare asked, getting increasingly annoyed at all the obfuscation.

'David didn't tell you in the sitting room?'

'Not really.'

'How interesting. I wonder why that is. He must want to see your instinctive reaction. Are you easily shocked?'

'No.'

'Let's see.' Celeste stooped slightly, as she was taller than Clare, took her chin in her fingers and kissed her lightly on the lips, her tongue darting out into Clare's mouth in the briefest of intrusions.

Clare was so surprised she barely reacted at all. The woman took this to be a green light and kissed her a second time more forcefully, this time using her hand to squeeze Clare's left breast.

'Darling . . .' The Duke strolled over. 'You've started without me.' He put his plate down and stroked his wife's bottom. 'She's lovely, isn't she?'

'Apparently David still hasn't told the young lady why we're all here.'

The Duke laughed. 'He is naughty.' He looked at Clare, putting his hand on her upper arm and caressing it. 'We are here, how should I put it, because we have certain preferences which we like to indulge. Publicly. David got us all together. He's very clever when it's a matter of *oser*.'

Clare glanced across the room at Bridget. The American was talking to the blonde waif, though her companion had disappeared. As she watched Bridget touched the girl's mouth with her finger. The girl smiled. Presumably Bridget had been told what was going to happen and had no objection to the idea. Nor any, judging from the way she pulled the blonde into her arms and kissed her on the mouth, to lesbian relationships.

'And what is David's preference?' Clare said coolly, not at all sure which of the two emotions she was experiencing – horror and fascination – was going to predominate. She could still feel Celeste's tongue darting between her lips.

The Duke smiled. 'I'm sure you know that already. It's very much the same as mine. But he's going first tonight.'

'Going first?'

'Follow us,' Celeste said. She put down her plate, most of her desserts uneaten, and took Clare's hand, like the spider who had chosen to escort the fly personally into the web.

There was a small door at the far end of the dining room. Celeste opened it and led the way through. The corridor beyond was long, narrow and windowless, the only light coming from a single naked light bulb swinging from the ceiling. There was only one door off it at the far end.

Again Celeste opened the door, this time allowing Clare to go first. She found herself in a large room, the walls draped with long scarlet velvet curtains. Strewn across the red, carpeted floor were three or four rather old-fashioned sofas, upholstered in Dralon, and dotted with different-shaped cushions. There were two armchairs in the same material. All the seating faced the same wall, where a platform jutted out into the room, a miniature version of a stage in a theatre, complete with a bar of spotlights above it. On the 'stage' was a mattress and a prie-dieu consisting of a narrow rectangular box about three feet high, with a padded step at one side, for kneeling to pray. The top surface, where the elbows would rest, was padded too.

At the back of the room was a large walnut wardrobe. It had two doors and four large drawers. Beside it was a side-table laden with drinks, bottles of gin, brandy, whisky and vodka, red and white wine and a wine cooler containing champagne, as well as all the appropriate glasses. The room had a curious smell, a combination of woman's perfume and something Clare did not recognise, a musky heady scent.

'Make yourself at home,' the Duke said. He slumped on to one of the sofas while his wife poured herself a glass of wine.

The door had closed itself on a hydraulic spring. It was pushed open again by Anna, who led Bridget into the room.

'Very cosy,' the American said, glancing at Clare.

'She's not having you all to herself, is she?' Celeste asked.

'Not necessarily,' Bridget replied.

The Duchess sidled up to Bridget, then ran her hand down the American's body, digging her fingers into her crotch. She leant forward and kissed her on the mouth. Immediately Bridget embraced her, kissing her back ferociously, turning her head and mashing their mouths together, her hand slipping on to Celeste's chiffon-covered buttocks.

'What about me?' Anna said, pushing herself into Bridget's back and embracing both women.

'Are you feeling left out?' the Duke said, looking from the triad of women to Clare.

Clare was not at all sure what she was feeling. At least everything David had said to her earlier made sense now. He had misread the fact that she had made him attend to her needs so forcefully, last Friday, as an indication that her sexual preferences were as complex as his own, imagining she had been too inhibited to tell him what she really wanted. It was a triumph of twisted desire over commonsense, his optimism flying in the face of reality. How long he had been holding his soirees of like-minded individuals she did not know, but he had obviously taken her behaviour as an opportunity to introduce her to his more arcane rituals.

Bridget's presence and acquiescence had added additional spice to the proceedings as far as David and his friends were concerned, but additional complications for Clare. She had never heard the slightest hint on the company grapevine that Bridget was gay, or bisexual, but clearly that is what she was. The evidence was right there in front of her eyes.

Clare needed a drink. She poured herself a brandy and sat on one of the two armchairs. Watching the three women, their arms linked around each other, their mouths kissing and licking each other's mouths and necks, hands exploring their softly fleshed bodies, revived no memories of Andrea, or Liza for that matter. She felt no flash of excitement.

At that moment the lights in the room dimmed. She saw Anna lead Bridget over to one of the sofas, while Celeste joined her husband. The bank of spotlights above the stage lit up, bathing the whole area in bright white light.

Virginia Ansel marched out from the wings, the velvet curtains concealing a small doorway. She was wearing a black leather corset – her large breasts only just contained in the cups of its bra, her waist cinched in by its strong laces and heavy boning – and long black stockings, their welts stretched over her meaty thighs, clipped into short leather suspenders. She wore black calf-length boots with stubby heels, but was without panties. Buried deep between her gargantuan thighs Clare could see tufts of pubic hair. In her left hand she held a riding crop. Clare recognised it immediately. It was exactly the same type David had given her a week earlier.

David followed the woman on. He was naked apart from a pair of white satin, lace-trimmed French knickers, a pair he had worn with Clare several times. They were too small and the material was stretched tautly over his slender, girlish hips.

'Stand still,' the woman barked. He stopped dead in his tracks. 'Dirty boy,' she said. 'Aren't you?'

'Yes.'

'Naughty, naughty boy.'

Clare saw the outline of his penis in the satin beginning to unfurl rapidly.

'Yes.'

'All the trouble I have to go to for you.'

'Yes.' David's face was twisted by his excitement. Clare had seen that expression so many times, a combination of shame at how he was behaving and acute arousal.

'Get down, then. You know what I'm going to have to do.'

'Yes.'

Viscount Bonmouth knelt on the prie-dieu. The big woman came around the other side of it so she was facing him. She took his hair in her hand and wrenched his head up so he was staring into her enormous bosom.

'Kiss it,' she demanded. She pulled the front of the bra-cups down and her big breasts spilt out like melting ice cream. David reached forward and began licking and kissing the flesh.

Clare heard a moan of delight. She looked to her left and saw that Anne had slipped on to the floor in front of Bridget, who had squirmed the split skirt up over her hips so the girl could bury her face between the American's thighs. The light from the stage provided enough illumination for Clare to see the girl's tongue burrowing into the nylon tights.

When she looked back at the stage, Virginia had turned round, her large flabby bottom perched on top of the prie-dieu. David was licking it enthusiastically, covering every inch of flesh with his tongue.

Celeste got to her feet. She went to the wardrobe at the back of the room and opened one of its doors. Clare's eyes followed her. She saw a selection of whips, tawses and wooden paddles hanging from hooks screwed on to the inside of the door. There were several school-type canes with curved hands and a riding crop identical to the one Virginia was using. It was this that Celeste selected.

'Not good enough,' Virginia announced. David redoubled his efforts. The big woman leant forward, angling her buttocks up and allowing him access to her sex, its labia covered with curly black hair.

Thwack. The sound echoed across the room. The Duke was bending over the arm of the sofa, his trousers and pants around his knees, Celeste towering above him.

Bridget stood up. She unzipped her dress and peeled it off her body. Her tights followed and her white thong-cut panties. She positioned the blonde, who still sat on the floor, so her back was against the sofa, then walked forward straddling her body until her pubes were pressed against the girl's face. Then, forcing the blonde's head back against the seat of the couch, she knelt on the edge of it, pressing her sex down on to the girl's mouth.

Clare looked at the stage. Virginia was standing behind David with the whip raised in her right hand. She stroked it down on to his satin-covered buttocks. David gasped.

Clare felt very little. The emotions she had experienced earlier, both the horror and the fascination, had been replaced by a curious sense of calm. She saw it all now, David's whole plan. He had brought her here to show her, more explicitly than words could do, what he expected from her. He'd assumed last Friday had been his first glimpse of the tip of an iceberg that she had never revealed to him before – that she had, for once, asserted her own needs. But nothing could be further from the truth. Her reaction had been caused by a mixture of anger and sexual need, not by some strange desire. In the past Clare had gone along with his games purely because she had liked him, and, if she were honest, she liked the things he did to her. But that was not what she wanted from a man. Gary's arrival on the scene had made that perfectly clear to her.

In his twisted way she realised this performance had been like a proposal of marriage, a statement of what he wanted and what he was, a first step on what he hoped would be a meeting of minds.

Clare finished her brandy in one gulp.

Thwack. The sharp sound of leather on satin-covered flesh made her flinch.

She got to her feet. To her right the Duke of Tidmouth was on his knees, carefully licking his wife's high-heeled shoes. To her left Bridget was staring into space, seeing nothing, her hands crushed back against her own breasts, her body trembling in the throes of orgasm – the first, Clare was sure, of many.

Without a word, Clare opened the door. She walked through into the narrow, dingy hallway. The door closed noisily on its spring, making her jump. In the dining room she walked past the abandoned food and out into the vestibule. She opened the front door and slammed it after her.

The Daimler was parked a little way up the street. The driver spotted her and got out of the car, opening the rear passenger door.

'It's all right, I'll walk,' she told him.

And walk is what she did.

# Chapter Eight

---

*THE PHONE RANG* twice before she picked it up.

'Hello?'

'Clare?' It was Bridget's voice.

'Yes.'

'Are you busy?'

'No.'

'Have you eaten?'

'No. I thought you were going home today?'

'I stayed over. I'm scheduled on a flight on Sunday afternoon. Would you have dinner with me?'

Clare would have liked to say no. 'Of course.'

'Pick me up in half an hour.'

Having dinner with Bridget Goldsmith was not Clare's first choice for a Saturday evening. Her first, second and third choice would have been Gary Newby, especially after last night. What she had seen may not have excited her directly but it had left her with a desperate yearning for sex; not sex in general but sex in particular, sex with Gary. Going to bed with Gary, with all his energy and power, and his simple, uncomplicated sexual needs, would wipe away the slightly disorientated feeling she'd had all day. Like Alice, after inhabiting the world behind the looking glass, she found the real world distinctly odd.

After everything that had happened in the last week it was not a question of taking a moralistic stand. That didn't mean she hadn't been bruised by the experience. What made it worse was that she knew it was, at least in part, her fault. If she had refused, from the beginning, to join in with David's sex games they would not have escalated into the more serious ones, and he would have not imagined – for even a second – that Clare had sexual leanings similar to his own, and would never have invited her to attend a meeting of the Society of *Oser*.

Clare looked at her watch and went upstairs to change. She supposed spending the rest of the evening with Bridget was better than spending it on her own, endlessly dwelling on the events of last night and cursing Angela and Angela's magazine.

She had a quick shower in her new cubicle and tried Gary's mobile phone once more. She called it three times already in the irrational hope that he'd finish early. The operator told her his phone was switched off.

Quickly she put on make-up and selected a dress, a simple stone-coloured, jersey strap-dress that left her shoulders and arms bare and had a knee length skirt. By the time she found the matching high-heeled shoes, Bridget's Daimler was drawing up outside.

The doorbell rang.

'Good evening,' she said.

'Hi, Clare.'

'Would you like to come in for a drink first?'

'Sure. The night is young.'

Clare led the way into the sitting room. As usual Bridget wore white, a loose-fitting silk shift. Her tights were flesh-coloured and shiny and she was wearing little white sandals.

'Hey, this is real nice. Very classy.'

'I've just had some work done. Things are not quite back to normal.' I'm not quite back to normal either, she thought but did not say.

'Looks fine to me.'

'What would you like?'

'Vodka rocks.'

Clare walked into the kitchen, the ranks of ash-fronted cupboards perfectly matched to the large terracotta tiles on the floor.

'Nice little garden too,' Bridget said, following her through.

Clare got ice from the fridge and knocked it out of the tray over the sink. She poured herself a gin and tonic, and handed Bridget a tall glass of vodka.

'Cheers,' she said. The American sat at the kitchen table, so she joined her.

'Cheers.' Bridget took a sip. 'Listen, I came here for a reason. Two reasons. You know me. I don't like beating about the bush.'

'So I gather.' From the look on Bridget's face the news didn't look good.

'The first is that I was out of line last night, way out of line. I got carried away. No excuses. I was always into history. Always had this thing about it. I suppose what with David and the Duke . . . it was like getting high. I was out of control.'

'You don't have to explain to me.'

'I think I do. I assumed you were into it too. I didn't realise . . . well if I had . . . The point is I

191

wouldn't like it to be known in the company what went on. I like to keep my private life private. Strictly private.'

'I understand. No one will hear it from me.'

'I like women, always have. Don't get me wrong, I like men too. Kinda swing both ways. Variety is the spice of life; that's what they say, don't they?'

'It's none of my business.'

'OK. Well, now that's out of the way. Second reason. Business.' She was looking at Clare intently. 'You run a tight ship, Clare. I'm impressed. I like the way you motivate your staff. I like your sales figures. I like your attitude. On the other hand I did *not* like what I saw in Paris. I've decided that the European launch should be handled in London as planned.' She paused for that information to sink in. 'I also want you to initiate a study into whether it would be possible to run the whole European operation from London. Cut out the French office first, say, then the German, Spanish, etc. Do you think you could handle that sort of responsibility?'

'If it was thought out and carefully planned.'

'Of course we'd have to work out a new remuneration package, share options, a seat on the main board.'

'Of course.' Clare tried to sound calm despite the fact she was being handed the opportunity of the biggest advancement in her entire career to date.

'Good. That's what I thought you'd say.' Bridget was smiling, a thin, weak smile but a smile nevertheless, her dark green eyes crinkled at the corners. 'So, do you mind if I ask you about David? I won't be offended if you tell me to go to hell.'

Clare's mind was still spinning with the

implications of what Bridget had said. She tried to snap it back into gear. 'Actually, I'd rather like to talk about it.'

'I love that.'

'What?'

'The way you say "actually". So English.'

'I suppose it is.'

'So what? You've had it with the Viscount now?'

'Yes. It was all my fault. I mean my fault it went so far. He obviously has very . . .' she searched for the right word '. . . exotic sexual needs, that I can't satisfy.'

'Can't or won't?'

'Won't.'

'But you must have known before last night?'

'Oh, I did. David had these little games he liked to play.'

'Like what?' Bridget asked eagerly.

'Oh, he used to buy me all sorts of lingerie – like me to get dressed up for him. Then he started to want to wear some of it himself. I thought it was harmless. To tell you the truth, I was never that interested in him to care too much what he wanted.'

'But you didn't know about the Society?'

'Not until last night.'

'Must have been a shock.'

'It was.'

'Do you think all aristos like to be whipped? The Duke had a go with Virginia after you'd gone.'

'We have caning at our best schools. Perhaps they get a taste for it.'

'Sure was interesting.'

Clare sipped her gin and tonic. Whether it was

due to the alcohol or Bridget's news, she was feeling very much better. The thought of going out to dinner was suddenly very appealing.

'God, just talking about last night is making me horny,' Bridget said. It was completely out of character. Clare had never heard her make any reference to herself, let alone to her sex life.

'You had a good time, I gather,' she said cautiously, not wanting to explore too far down that road in case Bridget took offence.

Apparently the American was in the mood for revelations. 'Between you and me, I had a very good time. That little blonde was a slut! Virginia had got her well trained.'

'And you like that?'

Bridget smiled again, an odd, crooked smile this time. 'It can be lonely at the top. I suspect you and I are similar in some ways. We're both very controlled. Very self-disciplined. We have to be. It's a hard world out there. Every so often it's necessary to let the reins slip. Some people do drugs. Or booze. Sex is my preferred option. I find it very easy to give myself up to sensuality. And there's something wonderfully wicked about doing it with another woman. It has one drawback, however.'

Clare realised Bridget hadn't asked her if she'd ever been with a woman. She wasn't at all sure what she'd have said. 'What's that?' she asked innocently.

'It always makes me horny for a man.'

'Really?' Clare breathed a sigh of relief.

'And how.'

Clare knew that feeling. After Liza she had wanted Gary desperately. On the other hand she *always* wanted Gary desperately.

'I suppose that's the difference between an amateur and a real dyke. Pity there's not such a thing as a male brothel. I could really use one right now. Men get all the breaks when it comes to sex, don't they?'

'I suppose so.' The conversation was making Clare feel horny too. She ached to feel Gary inside her again – that big, broad cock filling every inch of her. The thought made her squirm uneasily on the chair. 'So where do you want to eat?'

'You choose. It's your town.'

'I wonder . . .' The thought of Gary and Liza had made her think of the Key Club. As they were finally departing his loft, Malcolm Furness had told her that she was welcome at the club at any time. She only had to ring. she decided to see if he was as good as his word. 'Won't be a minute.'

She walked into the sitting room and picked up the phone book. She looked up the number and punched it into the phone.

'The Key Club. How may I help you?'

'Mr Furness, please.'

'Hold the line.'

'Mr Furness's office.' The voice was female.

'Is he there?'

'I'm sorry, he's not in at the moment. May I ask who's calling?'

'Clare Markham.'

'Yes, Ms Markham. May I help you with anything?'

'It's just Malcolm suggested the other night, if I ever wanted to use the club . . .'

'Certainly, Ms Markham. He mentioned it to me. Do you want to dine or dance?'

'I was hoping for a table for two.'

'What time?'

Clare looked at her watch. It was eight fifteen. 'Nine.'

'Table for two at nine. Just mention your name to the man on the door. I'll make all the arrangements.'

'That's very kind of you.'

'Our pleasure. And I'll tell Malcolm you rang.'

'Would you? Thank you.'

'Not at all.'

Clare smiled as she put the phone down. Taking Bridget to the Key Club would be another feather in her cap, though from what had just transpired she hardly needed one. More over, it was always possible that after his long and arduous day posing for photographs Gary might decide to drop into his old friend's club for a drink.

'Clare Markham,' Clare told the burly bouncer with the gold teeth, who was holding back the queue that seemed to be a permanent feature outside the Key Club.

The doorman smiled. 'Yes, Ms Markham, right this way please.' He unhooked the red cordon and ushered them through. Bridget looked suitably impressed.

The girl in the tight, gold leotard behind the desk had also been briefed. 'Good evening, Ms Markham,' she said before Clare could announce herself. 'Please go straight through, no need to sign in. Mr Furness has taken care of everything.'

Clare led the way into the bar. The *maître d'*, in her pastiche of a man's evening dress, wished them good evening and showed them to the same corner table Clare had occupied with Gary. She told them that Mr Furness would like to offer them a bottle of champagne or anything else they would care for. They settled for champagne.

Over dinner they discussed business. Fortunately Clare had given a lot of thought to the integration of the whole European operation. It would represent considerable savings in costs and manpower, and she explained her ideas of how it could be achieved with the least disruption. Bridget listened carefully, making pertinent points with her usual bluntness while she demolished a large entrecôte steak, a plate of potatoes and a double portion of pear and almond tart with whipped cream – one appetite, perhaps, being used to slake another.

'It seems like you're already ahead of the game on this,' Bridget said, as the desserts were cleared away and the waiter brought *demi-tasse* cups of expresso coffee.

'It always seemed like a logical progression. I wasn't going to bring it up until after you'd made the decision on the launch. The idea could work equally well if it were based in Paris.'

'With Claude? I don't think so. I wasn't impressed with his arguments on the commercials.'

'He was on your side.'

'True. But you convinced me we were wrong. The greatest asset of management should be the ability to listen. Anyway, that's enough business. In the absence of a male brothel, what do you suggest we do now?'

For a moment Clare wondered if Bridget was going to proposition her. She dismissed the idea at once. If Bridget was concerned with anyone in the company being told about her sexual proclivities, she certainly wouldn't want to compromise herself by sleeping with one of the senior executives.

'It's a funny thing, isn't it? Women have caught up with men in a lot of ways. I mean we run companies, do deals. Pay for our own dinner. Have more heart attacks. But we still can't go out and rustle up a man like a man can go get a woman. I mean, if you go up to a guy in a bar and tell him you want to get into his pants they either think you're a serial killer with a vendetta against men, or a hooker.'

'It's changing a bit.' She thought of Gary. She had definitely taken the lead in that situation.

As the waiter poured the last of the half-bottle of dessert wine they'd ordered (with Bridget's chauffeur-driven Daimler outside they didn't have to worry about driving), Clare spotted a familiar face walking towards their table.

'Clare. Well, you look terrific.'

Malcolm Furness towered above them, his bulky body clad in a black evening suit, a yellow bow-tie and matching cummerbund. He took Clare's hand and stooped to kiss her on the cheek but his eyes were riveted on Bridget.

'Malcolm Furness, Bridget Goldsmith,' Clare said. 'This is Malcolm's club.'

'Pleased to meet you.' Bridget smiled, extending her hand.

'And you. May I join you?'

'Sure,' Bridget said.

A waiter was summoned to pull up another chair.

'Thanks for arranging all this,' Clare said. 'It was really nice of you.'

'No problem. I'm glad you came. Everything OK? If it wasn't, I'll have the person responsible taken out and shot.'

'It was just perfect,' Bridget said. 'Love it here.'

'Thank you. Sorry I wasn't in earlier. Had to go to dinner with one of my investors. Boring old fart. He thinks 'cause he's got money in the place he's got the first choice of all the girls who work here.'

'Some of the girls are very attractive,' Bridget said. 'Especially the *maître d'*.'

'You're very attractive,' Malcolm said bluntly.

'Thank you. I'm very glad you think so.'

'How about some more wine? Or some champagne?'

'That's a great idea,' Bridget said.

Malcolm signalled to a waiter who appeared to know what he wanted without being told.

Bridget was leaning forward, her elbows on the table, staring at Malcolm, her eyes wide open, her whole attitude subtly changed, her body language suggesting a receptiveness and softness that were not characteristic. The Chief Executive of KissCo had melted away to be replaced by a much less daunting animal. Perhaps, Clare thought, when it came to men that was a trick she should try to learn.

'You know, you've got a lovely mouth, Malcolm,' she said.

'My friends call me Mal.'

'Are we going to be friends? I do hope so.' She touched his arm and batted her eyelids.

'Yeah, right.'

The waiter arrived with a bottle of Dom Perignon. He opened the bottle noiselessly and poured the wine into three glasses before crushing the bottle back into a bucket full of ice.

'Well, cheers!' Malcolm said, picking up his

glass. 'I hope you'll come again.' He was still looking at Bridget.

'Bridget's off to Houston in the morning.'

'Really. Houston. I've never been there.'

'You'll have to come over. I'm sure we could show you a very good time.'

'I'm sure you could. As long as you gave it your personal attention. What time's your flight?'

'Don't worry, I don't have to get up early.' If she had made her interest in Malcolm any more obvious, Clare thought, she would have been sitting in his lap.

'Are all Houston women so up front?' he asked.

'Oh dear, am I scaring you? We were just talking about that, weren't we Clare? How women have to wait for a man to make the running. I mean, I can't say to you that I'd love you to take me to bed, can I? Wouldn't be ladylike.'

'I thought you just had,' Malcolm countered. He was grinning from ear to ear, but not smugly.

'Ask him to show you his loft,' Clare said. She decided she could get to like Bridget. She admired her directness.

'Your loft?'

'Yeah. Upstairs. You want to see it?'

'Only if it's got a large bed. Otherwise let's go to my hotel.' She squeezed his arm. 'I'm sorry, is this putting you off? I know a lot of men find assertive women a big problem. They can't get it up or off, whichever.'

'Both probably,' Clare said with a smile. Bridget's attempt to shed her executive role hadn't lasted long. Perhaps she'd sensed it was not a part she needed to play with Malcolm.

'You're quite a lady,' he said.

'What makes you think I'm a lady?'

'Let's go then. Have you seen Gary?' for once he turned to look at Clare.

'Gary?' Just the sound of his name sent a shock-wave down to her sex. Clare was clearly in the same state as Bridget.

'Yeah. He called me about ten. Said he was coming over.'

'Here?' Clare said in disbelief. She couldn't believe her luck.

'Yeah.'

'Who's Gary?' Bridget asked. Her fingers were drawing delicate patterns on the top of Malcolm's hand.

'A friend of mine,' Clare told her.

'Another viscount?'

Malcolm laughed. 'Gary's a prince among men but he ain't no lord. We're both from the other end of the social ladder. We went to school together.'

'Well, I haven't seen him,' Clare said.

'Perhaps he's upstairs.'

Clare looked puzzled.

'In the flat. He's got a key,' Malcolm explained. 'He can use it whenever he likes. Come on, let's go and see.'

They got up. Malcolm grabbed a passing waiter. 'Have the booze sent up, there's a good boy,' he said.

'Certainly, Mr Furness.' The waiter collected the bottle from the table.

'Shouldn't waste good champagne, should we?' He took Bridget's arm. 'I've got a dumb waiter from the kitchens right up to the flat. Handy if I ever fancy anything.'

They walked down to the disco. It was full, *Saturday-Night-Fever* full. A gyrating mass of people danced to music so loud it was at the absolute limit of tolerance of the human ear; the heat extreme too, most of the dancers' clothes soaked with perspiration that was evaporating to give the room the air of a sauna.

They travelled up in the lift. Though the space was limited, it was no accident that Bridget's body was pressed against Malcolm's.

Malcolm took out his key and unlocked his front door.

'Be it ever so humble,' he said, throwing the door open and indicating that the women should go through.

The lights in the loft were already on. As before, the lighting was selective. The lights around the kitchen and the four sofas in the middle of the room were all off, but the halogen spotlights that illuminated the far side of the room, where the large double bed was, were burning brightly. And their bright white light revealed a startling and startled tableau. Kneeling on all fours on the bed was a long-haired, big-breasted blonde. She was naked, her breasts hanging down to brush the cream sheet that covered the mattress. At the back end of her long body a man was kneeling behind her, his navel butting against her buttocks, his penis quite obviously buried in her sex. He was a black man, his body delineated by groups of muscles, each one separate and distinct like an anatomical chart of the human form. At the other end of the blonde was a white man, almost equally well-endowed in terms of his physique. He was standing at the edge of the bed, his fingers laced into the blonde's hair, most of his cock firmly held in her mouth. The woman's long, straight and slender back formed a sort of bridge between the two men.

The tableau was frozen. For a moment no one moved.

Clare recognised them all. The blonde was Angela Barker. The black man was the male stripper from the pub. The white man was Gary. An intimate little threesome.

'Well, look at that,' Bridget said, almost under her breath. 'It's not only the aristos who know how to have a good time!'

Gary was the first to react. He pulled out of Angela's mouth. Under the bright lights his cock was shiny with Angela's saliva. As there were no lights on by the front door he was straining to see who had come in.

'Is that you, Mal?'

'Yes, and me,' Clare said. She walked over to the bed, her high-heels clacking on the wooden floor where it was not covered with rugs. '*Me*' she repeated, brazenly sitting on the bed by her friend. 'Hi, Angie, having fun? I didn't know this was the sort of shoot you had in mind.'

'Clare! Hell, where did you come from?' Angela said.

'I thought you might need some help. Don't let me interrupt, please,' she added, looking up at Gary.

'Hi,' he said weakly.

'What is all this?' the black man said, impatient, no doubt, to get on with what he'd already started.

Clare's emotions were complex. She felt angry with Angela. She also felt jealous. But her overriding emotion at that moment, seeing Gary standing there, with his magnificent weapon sticking out in front of him like the lever that operated a machine, was a quite inordinate lust. There would be time for anger later, but not with Gary. She did not own him. They had made no vows, plighted no troths. Her feelings about Angela were a different matter, but they would have to wait.

She looked up at the stripper. She remembered his hard body and the sheen of his very black, hairless flesh, like the nap of finest silk. It excited her. The contrast between the colour of his skin and Angela's made the blonde look deathly pale.

'He's been on the shoot with us,' Angela volunteered. 'I used them both.'

'So I see.'

Her anger flared momentarily, then died away. In another situation she might have seen Angela's actions as a betrayal. But Angela knew how she felt about Gary, that it was lust not love. And Angela had always been more prone to act on impulse. Presumably the same impulse had applied when it came to the black stripper.

Clare had a choice, at least in theory. She could turn and walk out of the door. She was getting good at righteous indignation. But this situation was completely different from last night. Last night her sexual excitement had been virtually non-existent. Her fascination had turned to disgust, well at least to total disinterest, very early on. Not for one moment had she wanted to snatch the whip out of Virginia's hand and set about David, or, for that matter, bid for the attentions of the waif-like blonde. Tonight, however, her sexual arousal had already been primed. In the few short minutes since she'd walked through the door it had increased exponentially, humming now with a power she simply could not control. This was exactly what she'd wanted after all – well, almost exactly.

'Come here,' she said to Gary in a school ma'amish tone that David would have loved.

Gary stood in front of her, his erection inches from her face. 'Are you cross?' he asked sheepishly.

She leant forward, ran the tip of her tongue over his glans, then sucked his cock into her mouth until it was embedded in her throat, as a way of giving him an answer.

He moaned. He moaned again when Clare sucked hard, dimpling her cheeks with the effort and feeling his cock throb.

'You want me to go?' the stripper said.

'No,' Angela said quickly. 'You stay right where you are.'

The stripper grinned. He gripped Angela's fleshy hips and began moving in and out of her as he'd been doing before they were interrupted.

Clare decided she wanted that too. She wanted it very much. She pulled her mouth away from Gary's cock and stood up. The stone-coloured jersey dress slipped to the floor, both men watching her.

She suddenly remembered Bridget and looked around for her. The rest of the loft was dark and she couldn't see what had happened to Malcolm and Bridget. There was one thing she was sure of, however. After last night she knew Bridget was not likely to be easily shocked.

Gary came up behind her. He sunk his mouth into her neck, making her skin pimple. His hands slipped under the cups of her white satin bra, pushing it up over her breasts, then cupping them – pressing her nipples between the sides of his fingers. His erection was nestling into the nylon-covered curves of her buttocks.

'Sorry,' he whispered in her ear.

'Don't say you're sorry,' she said. 'Just fuck me, Gary. I need it.'

His hands slid down the sides of her body. He hooked his thumbs into the waistband of her tights and pulled them down over her thighs. Dropping to his knees behind her, he rolled the nylon down to her ankles then raised each of her feet in turn, pulling off her shoes and stripping the nylon away.

'Bend over,' he said quietly. She unclipped her bra and threw it aside before she did as she was told, then bent at the waist, her hands on the mattress, her legs straight. His mouth pressed into her buttocks. She wormed her feet apart, her thighs opening, allowing him deeper. His tongue explored the hole of her anus, then dipped into her vagina. It was her turn to moan. His tongue felt hot. It probed remarkably deeply.

Clare looked across to Angela. Their faces were not more than a foot apart. The ecstasy in the blonde's expression excited her. She looked up at the black man but he was not looking at her. Instead his eyes were locked on Angela's buttocks, watching his pummelling cock sliding in and out between her pursed labia.

Almost unconsciously Clare pushed her buttocks up, changing the angle of her sex, and making Gary's tongue flip from the mouth of her vagina up to her clitoris. It was swollen. He licked it enthusiastically, pushing it up and down with the tip of his tongue.

Clare felt her body shudder with sensation. It seemed to be so much more impressionable now, more susceptible to the slightest contact. After only a few seconds of this treatment she felt the first trills of orgasm running through her nerves.

'No,' she said. She didn't want that. She tore herself away. Clare climbed on to the bed and rolled over on to her back, opening her legs and bending them at the knee, holding her arms out for him.

The invitation was obvious. Gary did not need to be told what to do. He lay down on top of her, his big erection crushing into her labia. As she wrapped her arms around his back and thrust her legs up into the air, he raised his hips and plunged into her. Clare gasped. The unique sensation he inspired flowed through her again, her sex filled, satiated, complete.

'Oh god, Gary. That's wonderful,' she whispered in his ear.

'I know.'

Gary's cock buried inside her body was exactly what she wanted. It succeeded in wiping away everything else. The unpleasantness of last night was forgotten. David was forgotten. Clare closed her eyes. The feelings he generated were so strong, so tangible, they invaded every part of her. They were like a mud bath; she could wallow in them. But not for long. The thick, warm, fuzzy sensations turned, in seconds, to sharp, hot, luminescent need, creating and demanding a more acute form of satisfaction. As Gary pressed up into her, arching his body to concentrate his whole effort into penetrating her more deeply, Clare's body arched too, pushing against his weight as the intensity of orgasm shot through her.

She opened her eyes as she heard Angela gasp.

The stripper was imitating Gary, not pounding into the blonde but pulling her back on him while he used all his strength, his map of muscles rigid with the effort, to push his cock more deeply into her. Angela's eyes were open, but they saw nothing, glazed over and unfocused, her breasts quivering, her long blonde hair twisted and dishevelled.

The lights had been turned on in the middle of the room where the four sofas formed a square, and a movement caught Clare's eye. A foot came into view over the back of one of the sofas. It was still shod in a white sandal. As she watched she saw the crest of a man's buttocks appear then disappear again instantly. Clearly Bridget's newly discovered passion for Malcolm Furness had come to rapid fruition, so rapid they had not bothered to remove her tights, some other arrangement made to allow access.

Gary began to move inside her, his big cock sliding in and out of the slippery tube of her tight vagina. Every thrust was a symphony of pleasure, different tunes played in different chords but all with the same pounding tempo. Clare could feel his cock swelling and throbbing too, every inch of it thrilling her. He was going to come. Had she arrived a few minutes later it would have been Angela, not her, who would have been granted the pleasure of his ejaculation.

She wasn't sure whether everything that was going on around her was an added excitement or a distraction. Would she have rather been alone? She couldn't work that out. There was no doubt that watching Angela *in extremis* was exciting her. In all the time she had known Angela she had never made the connection before, but now, seeing her long blonde hair sweep across the bed, as her head swayed from side to side, she suddenly reminded her of Andrea. That thought needed to be worked on too. Would she like to push Gary aside and see how Angela would react if she tried to kiss her? The world, it seemed, was full of possibilities, endless permutations, implications and consequences.

In fact she soon realised there was only one thing she wanted to feel. She raked her fingernails down Gary's back. Her left hand worked down into his buttocks until she found the opening of his anus. Without hesitation she stuck her finger into it, twisting it around and pushing it in as deeply as she could. The intrusion caused a violent spasm in his cock. Clare found his ear with her mouth and stuck her tongue deep into the inner whorls. Another wild jerking. His cock reared deeper into the velvety glove of her sex.

'Give it to me, Gary, don't make me wait!' She sounded like the star of some cheap porno film, but she didn't care.

She twisted her finger again. Immediately his cock kicked twice in rapid succession and she felt his spunk, hot and sticky, jetting out into the depths of her sex. Her own body reacted as it always had, a tight ball of feeling locking every muscle and straining every sinew, pure concentrated pleasure arching through her, followed by another sensation almost as strong and certainly as sensual – the melting, delicious pleasure as her orgasm released its grip and she was left, seemingly floating in mid-air. Despite everything that was happening around her, for that moment she was only aware of herself and Gary, their bodies wrapped around each other tightly, his softening cock at the core of her, where a damp, warm wetness was already beginning to trickle out.

She was also aware, after that moment has passed, of another sensation, one that revived all her sexual energy, and exhilarated her like nothing else. Gary's cock was moving inside her again, subtly sawing up and down. As it did, she felt it swelling, hardening again, ready for more.

It was raining. The hot weather had broken with a thunderstorm. It had rolled around all afternoon, forked lightning streaking the sky, and sheets of rain bouncing up off the ground, guttering overflowing with water, unable to cope with the volume. In between the cloudbursts thunder rattled the windows, so loud it sometimes seemed to be right overhead.

Clare sat in her new kitchen, watching the rain run off the new windows. She was tired. She hadn't wanted to know what time it was when Bridget's Daimler had dropped her off at her house last night, but, to make matters worse, when she had finally got to bed she had been unable to sleep. Everything that had happened to her whirled around in her head, just like the thunderstorm was doing now.

It had been a roller-coaster ride. Having got on the train, it had travelled too fast to enable her to get off. It had looped and spiralled and plunged through unknown and dangerous territory under its own momentum. But last night it had ground to a halt and, a little unsteadily, Clare had finally staggered to her front door and, with a sense of relief, shut it against the world.

In the small hours, watching as the first tendrils of light found the gaps in the curtains at her bedroom window, she experienced a whole panoply of emotions. Anger. Disgust. Excitement. Regret.

She went from being angry with herself for not having turned and walked out of Malcolm's loft as soon as she'd seen what was going on, to being so sexually excited at the memories of what had happened that her whole body came alive, her nipples stiffened, her sex moist. She experienced disgust and revulsion at what she had seen – at what she'd allowed herself to participate in – followed instantly by regret that she had not done more, that she had not had the courage to take the black stripper or pursue the desire she had felt to see if the experiment with Liza could have been repeated with Angela. She regretted, more than anything, that she'd told Gary she was tired and wanted to go home alone.

It was all very confusing and lack of sleep didn't help. She couldn't work out whether she was angry with Gary or not. She supposed if there was anyone to blame it was Angela. She *was* angry with Angela. She'd lied to her, a lie of omission admittedly, but a lie nevertheless. She hadn't told her about the black stripper being used in the photo-shoot because that might have tipped her off to Angela's plans for extra-curricular activities after the shoot. Nor, she suspected, had Stickshift been involved. That was just a hastily concocted excuse to keep her away. Though it might have been Gary's idea to use the loft, Clare was sure Angela would have had another plan up her sleeve if they had not been going there.

All these musings were streaked with yet another consideration: Bridget's visit had been a success beyond her wildest dreams. Promotion to the main board was a coup and her career prospects had never looked better. However depressed she might be about her private life, that was a considerable consolation.

The phone startled her out of her reverie.

'Hello?' she said.

'Hi, Clare. It's B.' Bridget had never used that diminutive before. Did it indicate a new level of intimacy?

'Hello, how are you?'

'Ragged. What about you?'

'The same. Where are you calling from?' The line sounded a little hollow.

'The plane. I just wanted to thank you. You certainly know how to show a girl a good time! I'm going to have to return the compliment when you're over in Houston.'

Clare remembered what Bridget had said at David's house. She shuddered at the thought that she might be introduced to another Society of Oser. For the moment her orgy-quota had been filled.

'It wasn't planned,' she said quickly.

'Sure. Listen. That guy you were with, Mal's friend?'

'Gary.'

'Was that his name? What does he do?'

'He's a builder. He built my house extension.'

'Oh.' She sounded disappointed.

'Is there a problem?'

'I thought I heard the blonde mention something about a shoot. I thought he was a model.'

212

'First time. She works for a magazine. They picked him for an assignment on men's suits.'

'Great! Get some copies of the photographs, will you? Courier them to the States. Tomorrow if you can.'

'Why?'

'That new men's perfume we're doing. We need a new face. Don't you think he'd be perfect?'

The Zeal range of men's toiletries was a new product-line for KissCo, the first time they had ventured into the male domain. The fragrances had been developed and the packaging designed, but as yet the advertising agency had failed to come up with the right face to identify with the product. Naturally, as market research showed, men would only buy such products if they felt they would make them sexually irresistible so the man chosen had to be a hunk. Bridget was right. Gary was perfect. Better than perfect. Who was more sexually irresistible than him?

'You're right!' Clare said enthusiastically. 'He'd be sensational.'

'So you'll get on to it?'

'I'll get the pictures tomorrow morning. Meantime I'll get him into our people and do some shots we can e-mail on the computer.'

'Great. Have fun. See you in Houston.'

Clare didn't hang up. She punched in Gary's number. There was no reply.

She tried again after half an hour. Still no reply. She wondered if he might be with Angela. They had apparently gone their separate ways last night, but at the moment she wouldn't put anything past her friend. Perhaps she had both men in her bed and was giving them a repeat performance. She punched her number into the phone.

'Hello?'

'Angela.'

'Hi Clare.' Her voice sounded subdued, expecting trouble. 'Listen, I know what you're going to say.'

'I'm not going to say anything,' Clare said, surprised that the sound of her friend's voice had wiped away any animosity.

'It was just an impulse, that's all. You know me.'

'Forget it.' It was impossible to be cross with her.

'You know what a greedy girl I am.'

'Is he there now?'

'Who, Gary? God no.'

'Or Mr Macho?'

'It was just a one-off.'

'Where did you find him, by the way?'

'Who, the stripper? These people have agents. I just called his agent.'

'Does he look good in a suit?'

'Hmm . . . better without, don't you think? Weren't you tempted?'

'No – yes – no.'

'Let's have lunch tomorrow. My treat.' Angela wanted to build bridges.

'Great. Usual place. And, Angela, can you bring the photos from the shoot?'

'What for?'

'They'll be ready, won't they?'

'Yes.'

'I'll explain tomorrow.'

'See you then,' Angela said, sounding a little puzzled.

The doorbell rang as she put the phone down. At the same time there was another cloudburst.

Rain poured out of the sky in huge drops, bouncing noisily off the patio outside the window.

Clare opened the front door. In the short journey from his car to the door Gary had been soaked. He stood on the front path with rain running down his face, his T-shirt already transparent from the wet.

'Hi,' he said.

After the conflicting emotions she experienced last night, Clare had expected her reaction to seeing him to be mixed. It was not. Last night, despite the fact that his erection had been buried in another woman's mouth, her desire for him had been overwhelming. She felt the same reaction now.

'You're soaked,' she said.

'It would be nice if you'd let me in.'

She stood aside and let him into the hall, closing the door behind him.

'Wasn't sure I'd be welcome.'

'You're not.' She threw her arms round his neck and stretched up to kiss him on the mouth. She kissed him passionately, hungrily, as though she hadn't had sex with him for weeks. 'I never want to see you again,' she said, before crushing her lips against him once more. His tongue invaded her mouth. She sucked on it. It was hot and wet and made her body feel weak.

'Yeah, I can see that,' he said, breaking away. Effortlessly he hooked his hand under her knees and scooped her up into his arms.

'Never,' she said, as he carried her upstairs. 'I despise you. You disgust me.'

He strode into her bedroom. She kissed him again, gnawing on his lips, gnawing on his tongue.

'You'd better throw me out, then,' he said,

lowering her on to the bed.

She was wearing a baggy white T-shirt and a pair of white panties. He caught hold of the bottom of the T-shirt and pulled it over her head. She wasn't wearing a bra. He pushed her back on to the bed and dropped his mouth to her left breast, sucking on her nipple.

'I am going to throw you out, you animal. You can't possibly imagine I ever want to have anything to do with you again.' She struggled to sit up and attacked the belt of his jeans. Unzipping his fly, she freed his cock. It was erect, big and hard. She felt it throb as she curled her hand around it and squeezed it as tightly as she could. Her own sex was melting, so wet she was sure her juices were already soaking her panties. She had never wanted anyone as totally as she wanted him.

'You only want me for my body, don't you?' he said.

'Of course.'

He pulled the crotch of her panties aside. Once again there was no time to get undressed. The need was too urgent, too all-consuming. He threw her back and plunged his cock into her, filling her, giving her the instant gratification she only ever experienced with him.

'Just a bit of rough, that's all you want,' he said between clenched teeth, his cock powering into her, breaking the secret barrier in her sex, and ploughing beyond it.

'Yes, rough trade,' she managed to moan as she felt her vagina contracting around his erection, her body quickly giving into the inevitable.